T0284306

GRAPEFRUIT MOON

Shirley-Anne McMillan

Little
Island
Books create waves

GRAPEFRUIT MOON

First published in 2023 by
Little Island Books
7 Kenilworth Park
Dublin 6W
Ireland

First published in the USA by Little Island Books in 2024

Original translations of poetry by
Federico García Lorca © Ian McMillan

A British Library Cataloguing in Publication record for this book is
available from the British Library.

Cover illustration by Ana Jarén
Cover design by Anna Morrison
Copy-editing and proofreading by Emma Dunne
Typeset by Rosa Devine
Printed in the UK by CPI

Print ISBN: 978-1-91507-142-2
Ebook ISBN: 978-1-915071-52-1

Little Island has received funding to support this book from
the Arts Council of Ireland/An Chomhairle Ealaíon

10 9 8 7 6 5 4 3 2 1

To Ian
Muchas gracias, mucho amor x

Poesía, pequeño pueblo en armas contra la soledad
Poetry, a small town in arms against loneliness

– Javier Egea

Translated by Ian McMillan

PART ONE

September–December

1. Charlotte

Sixth form. A new start.

Walking into the student centre, I glanced around for Lucy and Artie. There they were, at the back. I tried to ignore Adam as I walked past him, but my eyes locked with his for a second by accident. He smirked and raised a hand in mock greeting.

His little gang of Stewards were gathered around him, their badges gleaming in the sunlight, bright as their futures — the elite, the rugby boys, the chosen ones. But the chosen ones were always boys, never girls. Welcome to the twenty-first century at one of Northern Ireland's best schools.

Not that I wanted to be a part of their group. Idiots. *Ignore them*, I thought. *Look, your friends are here. Ignore him.*

Adam hadn't been in touch all summer, and maybe he'd gotten over everything now. I shook off the thought of him.

Artie was in good form. He gave me a massive hug and scooched over so I could sit on the table next to him.

'Hey, new boy!' he called, looking over my shoulder.

I looked behind me, and sure enough, there was someone new standing at the window, looking a bit dazed. I couldn't blame him. Cooke's can be a lot if you're not used to it. It's like a little planet all of its own. You can forget you're in Belfast sometimes.

'Come and sit with us!' Artie went on as the boy acknowledged him. 'What's your name?'

'Andrew.' The new boy ambled over to us and leant against a desk. 'Drew, just.'

Lucy grabbed my arm, beaming. 'Sooooo,' she said, 'please say you decided on English in the end?'

'Yes. Also Sp–'

'Oh, yay!' said Lucy. 'What about you?' she said to the new boy.

'Um. No, not English. Spanish, though, and –'

'Cool!' I said. 'You'll love Don Antonio – he's brilliant.'

'Wooooo,' said Artie. 'Does someone have a little crush on señor teacher?'

'An intellectual one, maybe!' I said. 'Besides, I think you're more his type.'

'I'm everyone's type, darling,' said Artie, with a grin directed at the new boy, whose eyes widened.

'He's just teasing,' I said. 'Artie's a pussycat. Aren't you, Artie?'

'Miaow!' he purred, flexing a mock paw.

The bell rang and we headed off to form class. Turned out Drew was with me and Lucy, which was nice. We'd look out for him while he found his feet.

As I left the room, I noticed Adam staring at me. Urgh. At least I wouldn't have any classes with him. He was destined for a career in medicine, so it would be all science and maths for him. We'd hardly even see one another, and we only had two more years of school together. I was sure that everything was on the verge of settling down and disappearing into the new year ahead.

I was so completely wrong.

2. Drew

'Well?' Mum said. I'd barely put the second foot through the doorway. 'How was it, love?'

She had this rictus grin, like she'd been panicking all day, practising looking breezy when I came in. *Don't worry, Mum*, I thought. *I passed as human. I didn't let us all down.* Awk, that wasn't fair. She meant well.

'It was good,' I said, throwing my backpack on the kitchen chair.

And it had been OK. The students didn't seem too bad. Like, they were totally over-confident, though. And their humour ... It had no *edge* to it. All that sparkly enthusiasm was a bit hard to take. It was their total lack of sarcasm that really made me feel like the kid from the council estate – more than the thick carpets and the clean smell and the students driving up to school in their own shiny cars.

'I'm starving,' I said.

Her smile softened, like she'd finally breathed out after a full day of holding it in. 'I'll make you a sandwich. Go and get changed. And hang that uniform up! It cost more than —'

'More than a month's pay. I know.'

I knew she'd got a grant for the uniform. I saw the forms on the table one night before I went to bed. But I understood. They wanted me to value the opportunity I'd been given. Hardly anyone got into Cooke's sixth form from the outside, and nobody at all from our estate ever got in. Until I did. Walking out of our house in the morning it felt like that uniform was luminous against the dull grey houses. Like I was walking through Greenwood estate in a butterfly outfit. Everyone was looking. The neighbours even said, 'Congratulations, Drew!' as I passed. *Congratulations!* Not *Good luck!* Or *Have a good day!* But *Congratulations* – like I'd won the lottery or something.

I was halfway up the stairs when Dad came in.

'Drew!' he yelled, as if he was surprised to see me in our own house. 'Well? How was it?'

I stopped. 'It was good.'

'Great!' He beamed. 'That's my lad! You'll be at university next thing you know.'

No feckin' pressure, eh, Dad? I nodded at him and went up to my room.

I flipped open my laptop and switched it on while I went to the toilet. It always took about ten minutes to come on and I had to keep it plugged in cos the battery was wrecked.

At the start of Spanish class today, everyone opened their bags and pulled their iPads out. What the hell. I didn't know you were meant to have an iPad. It wasn't on the list of stuff to get before school. I must have looked like a total idiot staring at everyone tapping on their screens, not knowing what I was meant to do. Don Antonio smiled kindly and set one on my desk. I looked over at what Charlotte was doing. I pressed the button and all these little apps appeared in front of me. Charlotte noticed me swiping through them.

'Here, it's this one.' She tapped on the app that had the school crest. 'This is a school iPad, so it'll have all the subjects. When you download the app to your own iPad you can put in your student number and you'll just get the info for your subjects. Cool, eh?'

'Uh, yeah. Thanks.'

I was shitting myself, though. *Your own iPad*? Where was I gonna get an iPad from? I literally started imagining where I could get an iPad. I wondered if Jamie's ma still sold knock-off stuff. But even then. Maybe if I got a part-time job …

The teacher's voice woke me up. 'New student? Andrew?'

He had a Spanish accent and something about it made me relax a bit.

'OK. Well, welcome, Andrew.' He smiled and turned to the whole class and started talking about the A level curriculum. I had loved Spanish at my old school, Laney. Going over the words, saying them out loud when nobody else was in the house, it felt like knowing a secret code. I could write poems in Spanish and nobody even knew they were poems. It was like being invisible.

I hung up my uniform, put on my trackie bottoms and a T-shirt and flipped open a physics book. You would never have got homework on the first day at Laney. My phone beeped. Message from Dale.

> How's the posh school, genius? Comin down the rec later?

I flipped the book closed.

> Yeah. See you around 7.

The phone beeped again.

> Big news. Tell ye later.

3. Charlotte

You studying?

The buzz of Lucy's message made me jump. I *was* studying. Well, in between glances at Instagram. I'd got the latest iPhone the weekend before. A 'starting sixth form' gift from Mum. It was hard to leave it alone. Its perfectly rounded, shiny edges begged me to lift it. I looked at the Lorca poem on my desk. Don Antonio wanted us to translate it for tomorrow.

I got an A* in Spanish in my GCSE, but that was because Mum had hired a tutor. Couldn't have her little Lottie getting a B, could she? It would have been a big smudge on the string of A*s. That's how she thinks. Like everyone else I knew, I'd go on to university, and the idea of failure hadn't really occurred. That's just how it was at Cooke's. If you thought you were going to fail you were basically in the wrong place.

Yeah. Spanish.

I'd been looking at the poem for thirty minutes and so far had only translated the title: 'La Luna Asoma' – 'The Moon Rises'. Time for a short break? I closed the book and swiped my finger over the screen.

Two texts from Artie, something about some hot boy he saw on the way home. Two from Mum, sent during school, both about not forgetting to sign up for extra-curricular history. I answered Artie's message with a smiley emoji. I scrolled through Instagram. Lots of 'first day' selfies, some taken beside brand-new cars; Artie's deliberately vague references to fancying someone and a string of comments underneath with people trying to guess who; the usual memes.

Then I stopped scrolling. It was a picture of Adam sitting on a desk, feet on the chair in front of him, smiling up through his floppy fringe. He looked gorgeous. I had muted him on social media, but that didn't stop his picture popping up. New kids, younger kids, girls in our year. He was kind of a celebrity. I scrolled on, but I didn't feel like looking at my phone any more. I didn't feel like doing the Spanish either. I turned the lights out, put my AirPods in and lay on my bed, turning the music up loud.

The phone flashed light and dark. Lucy. I swiped the screen.

'Hiya,' I said.

'What's the craic? Have you finished that Spanish homework yet?'

'Nope. Translated the title. That's all. It's hard getting back into it. Have you done your homework yet?'

'Yeah, I did it earlier, when I got home.'

'Lick.'

'Here, did you see Adam this morning?'

Urgh. Why bring him up? But it had to happen at some point. Adam was the most influential sixth-former at Cooke's. He was also my ex-boyfriend. The likelihood of me getting through this year without someone mentioning his name in my hearing was zero.

'Yeah. He looked like a tosser,' I said sharply, hoping she'd take the hint. She did not.

'Looks like he's the new Stewards president.'

'Quelle surprise.'

'I know.' As if it was going to be anyone else. 'I saw him looking at that new kid, Drew. I wonder if he's going to be a Steward?'

'Urgh. Someone should warn him about those dickheads.'

'Come on, Lottie,' she said. 'They're not that bad. I mean, I know you fell out with Adam pretty majorly ...'

Understatement of the year. Adam wasn't happy when I'd ended it. 'You'll regret this,' he'd said. That's all. Just 'You'll regret this.' I had always known he had a mean streak. He'd make nasty comments about other people. Never about me, but sometimes he'd give me this look if I had my hair done a different way. He could let you know what he thought without even saying anything, which made it hard to complain. If you told him you felt uncomfortable, he'd tell you it was all in your mind. But that was in the past. I didn't want to go back there. He could be someone else's problem now.

'Adam's an idiot,' I said. 'And the Stewards are idiots. And I hope new Drew stays away from them.'

The conversation was becoming exhausting. The Spanish translation seemed almost appealing.

'But Charlotte. He might *need* them, mightn't he?'

I knew what she meant. Drew was poor. It was obvious, not only from the school that we all knew he'd come from, but also because of what had happened in Spanish when Don Antonio asked us to get out our iPads. The look of panic on his face. And I guessed that Lucy was right. The Stewards could probably help him. I mean, most of the school depended on them to set the social standard, to let people know their roles. What hope did someone from Greenwood estate have without them on his side?

'Yeah, you're probably right,' I said. 'I'd better go and do this translation.'

'Adios, amiga!'

I went back to my desk and switched on the lamp. It reflected in the window, a large silver orb below the small circle of the moon watching over the city.

The Moon Rises

When the moon rises

The bells are lost

And the paths appear

Impenetrable

I wrote a note at the side of the page. *Things look different at night-time.* That was true for certain. *Things can be more confusing in the moonlight.* My eyes felt heavy. I closed the book. I'd finish it in the morning. I switched off the light and got into bed. It was the first time in my life that I'd gone to bed without finishing my homework.

4. Drew

Dale was standing under our tree at the rec, beside the bench. He was never sitting. I looked at him, smoking a fag with one hand, the other in his pocket, one leg jiggling as he inhaled deeply. Dale was always moving, never standing still. Even when he was just waiting for someone.

'All right?' I said, holding out my hand. He passed me the smoke.

'Aye. What's the craic?'

'Not much,' I said. 'Will we go round to Maccy D's?'

'No cash, mate,' he said.

'I've got some. I'll get you a burger.'

'Wooooo!' He faked a swagger. 'They give out money at that school too?'

I thought about the iPad that Don Antonio had set on my desk and a wave of worry moved across my thoughts. I gave Dale the fag back. 'Mum gave me a tenner this morning and I never used it. I think she was crappin' herself all day that the rich kids would kill me or something.'

'Sweet!'

We walked down the path towards the town. Well, I walked. Dale bounced along beside me like Tigger. I don't know where he got his energy from but he always had plenty of it.

'So, you gonna tell me this big news anyway?' I said, trying to sound casual.

'Oh aye! I forgot. Right. Listen … this is mental …'

'Just tell me!'

'Right. Right.'

We waited at the traffic lights and he turned to face me and grabbed my shoulders, looking me right in the eyes. 'Who, out of all of us, is the least likely to get a shag?'

'I dunno. You?'

He rolled his eyes. 'No, I mean it. Who never has a girl-friend, hardly ever, and he's totally square, and a bit of a dick, but dead on with it, but, like, dopey lookin' and ...'

I was laughing. The lights changed and I pointed to the green man. ''Mon.'

We crossed over.

He was talking about Jonny.

'Did wee Jonny get the ride then?'

'More than that!' He beamed, his face full of knowl-edge. It was like he didn't want to tell me – he was enjoy-ing being the one with the secret. We got to McDonald's and I swung the big door open.

'Don't tell me he has two women on the go,' I said, 'be-cause that I *really* won't believe.'

'Nope!' said Dale. He walked right up to the counter and made his order without thinking. 'Large chip and a cheeseburger, love.'

The girl at the desk didn't smile and moved her head very slightly towards me.

'Same here. Please,' I said.

We didn't say anything else until we were sitting down and Dale suddenly blurted it out, mid-burger-unwrapping. 'He's only gone and got someone up the duff!'

'What!' I stopped chewing mid-bite.

'I know! But it's fuckin' true. He's gonna be a daddy.'

'Fuck. Who is she?'

'Well, you'll not believe me.'

'*Who?*'

He finished chewing and swallowed. He took a breath and looked at me, the smile fading. 'It's Karen.'

Karen. *My* Karen? Couldn't be ... But I knew it was her by the look on Dale's face. I tried to shrug it off.

'Wow,' I said. 'Wouldn't have put those two together.'

'Ano, right?'

He took another bite of his cheeseburger and started rambling on about Jonny and when he reckoned the loss of his virginity might have happened. It wasn't quite a change of subject, but it was obvious he was trying to steer the story away from the part that I couldn't stop thinking about.

Karen.

I'd only broken up with her in April, and now she was having Jonny's baby? I couldn't take it in. I always knew the day would come when she'd start seeing someone else, and I thought I could handle that. I'd have a new school, maybe new friends by then. A new life. But this was beyond *moving on*. What the hell, Karen? Did you hate me that much?

I stuffed the burger into my mouth with so much force I almost choked on it. *Don't cry. Don't fuckin' cry in the middle of Maccy D's, in front of Dale.* I wiped at my eye.

'Mate,' said Dale, 'she's a skank. You're better off, aren't ye?'

'Yeah,' I said.

And thing is, I knew I was better off. What if it had been me getting her pregnant? Messing everything up? But still. The thought of her and Jonny ... and a baby? And she wasn't a skank. But I knew Dale was just trying to cheer me up. I looked at him.

'Fuck this,' I said. 'Wanna go down the towpath?'

Going down the towpath, to sit by the side of the river, was shorthand for *Let's go and get loaded*.

He shrugged.

'Seriously?' I said. 'You don't want to? Did they replace you with a robot at tech or something?'

'Sorry, mate. I have a thing in the morning – a test – to see if I can get extra help this year. I have to be awake, y'know?'

I nodded. It wasn't fair to expect Dale to always be there for me. It was harder for him. He failed everything in school and he really wanted to make a go of things this year. I knew he wanted a car really badly, and the tech course he was on would teach him to fix one and he could still get the dole, so he reckoned he could end up getting a wreck of a car by the end of the year and be able to fix it up. But he'd find that course hard. He wasn't used to studying.

It was different for me. I always found that stuff boringly easy. I didn't do the exam to get into grammar school because I wanted to go to school with my mates, but I aced my GCSEs without much trouble. I didn't like the idea of moving to Cooke's, but when my school said I should consider doing A levels I thought Mum was going to burst with pride. She immediately started talking about university and *careers* and stuff and, to be honest, the thought of it didn't bother me. I knew I wouldn't fit in at a posh grammar school, but at the same time I thought maybe it would give me an excuse to keep on writing poems. Everyone else was talking about tech courses and jobs and I was being told I could stay at school, learn more Spanish, maybe even think about moving to another place and doing a degree later on. It seemed far-fetched at the time, and anyway I could never afford university. But then Mum found out that Cooke's students got a chance to win a scholarship fund for university, and that was it. She was convinced I was going to go to Cooke's, ace everything, win that money and go to college. And I went along with it, because why not? I didn't have any other plans.

Now, sitting here with Dale, getting a mental image of Karen and Jonny and their wee kid, them pushing a pram, getting a flat ... I imagined Dale fixing his car, fixing other people's cars. Everyone in Greenwood growing up, moving on. Where would I be while they all got jobs and kids and *lives*?

'Earth to Drew? Come in, Drew?' Dale clicked his fingers in front of my face. 'Don't do a huff cos I can't go out.'

'I'm not,' I replied.

But he was smirking. 'Cans at the park on Friday?'

He scraped his chair back and I lifted the tray, moving towards the bin.

'Aye. Why not,' I said.

5. Charlotte

I hardly slept. Got out of bed at 5 a.m. and finished the translation and the other homework. I was thinking of the new boy and what Lucy had said about him becoming a Steward.

The Stewards were a tradition at Cooke's. A tradition which spanned decades. The sixth-formers ran the club and each year they admitted a handful of new members, people who fit the bill – the smart ones, or the sporty ones, or the super-rich ones. The elite. The perks of being in the club were mainly that you were *in the club*. You got invited to things. The teachers left you alone a bit more. If you were the club president or a member of the committee you'd definitely have mentioned it in your university application. Local business owners reserved the best work experience opportunities for Stewards. And you'd also have servants. No kidding. The kids in the junior school got major kudos for doing stuff for you – bringing you snacks at break time, running to the cafeteria for you at lunchtime, that sort of thing. They were happy to do it, especially the first-years, because the Stewards were like a famous pop group or something. Everyone wanted to be seen with them. Everyone wanted to *be* them. And those little kids knew that someday they'd be in the sixth and if they'd been 'contributing' to Steward culture over the years they'd stand a better chance of getting an invitation. There was no rule to say that girls couldn't be Stewards, but they never were.

This was the first year that a lower-sixth boy had been voted in as president. But everyone knew it was going to happen. Adam Bailey had been Steward material since birth. His dad was one of the top barristers in Northern Ireland and he practically owned the school, contributing a huge grant every year including a scholarship for a deserving student, which would pay for their university education. Every year that scholarship went to a Steward. You didn't *have* to be a Steward to get it. But it was always a Steward who got it. People had been talking about Adam as Steward president since the start of fifth.

'Your head's in the clouds this morning,' Mum said.

'Huh?'

'I've asked you twice now if you have hockey this term,' she said. 'Careful, your tie's getting jammy.'

I sat up straight and removed my tie from the untouched toast on my plate.

'Yes, hockey's on,' I said. Maybe it was a good time to broach the thing I'd been waiting to ask her about. 'I think I might take creative writing after school this term?'

'Writing? What, like, poetry?'

She was going to say no. I knew that. But I had to ask anyway. 'No, poetry club's at lunchtimes.'

'You go to poetry club?' She was still stacking dishes, but she had slowed down as if she was processing this new side to me that she hadn't known about.

'Yes, it's not a big deal. Just some friends talking about poems and stuff.'

'Don't say *stuff*, Charlotte. Use your words.'

I rolled my eyes behind her back. 'Anyway, creative writing's after school. Miss Robinson's taking it. It wouldn't interfere with my studies. Not if I ... dropped hockey.'

Mum stopped stacking the dishwasher and turned around to face me. 'No.'

That's all she said. She turned back to the dishes, jamming them into the slots slightly harder than before. I had wanted to drop hockey every year since junior school and she'd never let me. I'd been team captain for the last three years running. We had won all the major tournaments. It's not like I *hated* it. I just wanted to try something new.

'*Poetry*,' she muttered under her breath.

Seriously. She wanted me to excel in English, reading other people's poems. Reading Shakespeare. Writing essays. Taking part in public speaking and debating competitions. But people who wrote their own poems – real people who were alive now? That was beneath her. *That* was silly and childish. I wanted to ask her if she thought that when Shakespeare was writing sonnets his mum would've found him ridiculous too. But there was no point. We'd had the conversation about 'hobbies' a million times: I was allowed to take one extra-curricular class apart from study groups, plus piano lessons, and the rest of my life was going to be studying. And since we'd discovered how good I was at hockey, then that was going to be it. Because why do something you might fail at when you could do the same thing over and over again and win all the time? I envied the kids who would take part in school drama productions. I always thought I'd enjoy doing that. But it was never going to be for me.

I scraped the chair back and left half my toast on the plate.

'Better go or I'll be late. See you later,' I said.

'Bye, love,' said Mum, without looking up from the dishwasher.

I didn't say anything else; there wasn't any point.

It was drizzling slightly and the leaves were all stuck to the pavement. The huge trees lined either side of the road we lived on. They darkened the road, but the places where the sunlight got through made the slick leaves shine underneath my feet. I loved this street. The big houses with their black wrought-iron gates and CCTV cameras should have felt intimidating, but they didn't – not to me. We'd lived here my whole life. As I got closer to the end of the road I could see kids piling out of Greenwood estate in their Laney High uniforms. We'd always hear stories about the Laney kids: that one gave birth to a baby in the school toilets; that one was in prison for selling drugs; that there was a stabbing and one died. That last one was definitely true – it was on the news. I shuddered at the thought of it as I got closer. And then I saw a different uniform. Our uniform.

'Drew!' I called.

6. Drew

I turned around and so did half the estate. All the people piling on to the Laney bus stopped pushing one another and turned their heads to see who was calling my name. It was like a moment frozen in time. Then someone wolf-whistled and everyone laughed. *Oh God, please don't let them start shouting stuff.* I heard one of the little kids say something about a 'rich hoor'. His mates giggled. I walked over to Charlotte as quickly as I could without actually running.

'Hi, Charlotte! Let's walk on the other side of the road?'

'Erm, OK. Why?'

'Just trust me. Those kids are a pain in the arse. Come on.'

I wanted to take her arm to lead her across as quickly as possible, but I knew if I did it would be inviting more cat-calls. She took the hint and we crossed the road.

'Do you know them?' she said.

Of course I knew them. Everyone knew everyone. Even the people you weren't friends with – you'd know their name at least, what family they were from.

'Yeah. They're wee dicks, though.'

She nodded. I felt a bit like Judas. They were just kids like me. Bored kids. Everyone liked a new thing to look at, to think about, to talk about. I was the same. If it had been someone else with the hot girl calling their name I'd've been just as interested as they were.

We were close to the station before we spoke again. I didn't mind the silence. I was still thinking about what Dale had said about Karen. Karen and Jonny. Karen's baby. I'd been up all night thinking about it. We had Spanish first class and I hadn't done the translation. *Great start, Drew.*

'Have you done the Spanish?' I asked Charlotte when we were on the train. Stupid question. Of course she'd done it.

'Yes,' she replied. 'What did you think of it?'

'Uh ... it was OK.'

She smiled gently. 'Did you get it finished?'

'No.'

'You want to have a look at mine?'

And that's how I ended up copying the hot girl's homework on the train to Belfast on the second day of school. I made a few deliberate mistakes so it didn't look as though I'd copied. I felt like a total idiot. She clearly thought I hadn't done it because I was thick. I *was* thick, though. I knew I'd have to stop going out on weeknights if I was going to keep up with these kids who didn't think about anything else but homework.

I dotted the full stop as the train squealed to a halt.

'Thanks,' I said, handing her the book back.

I wanted to say sorry, that it wouldn't happen again, that I had understood the work but that I just hadn't bothered doing it.

'No problem,' she said, snapping her bag shut and flashing a brilliant white smile as we got up. 'Don Antonio's great but he's strict about homework. You don't want to start off on the wrong foot.'

'I appreciate it.'

As we walked into the school's carpark there were several kids getting out of cars. It looked weird, kids getting out of cars in their school uniform. I didn't know anyone who was still at school who had a car. Charlotte waved to someone getting out of the passenger side of another student's car. She skipped towards him. I didn't know whether to follow her. We had travelled together, but I didn't know if she'd want me actually hanging around with her. I decided to walk on by myself. The guy who'd gotten out of the car was the boy who'd made that crack about Charlotte fancying the Spanish teacher. Arnold or something.

'Drew!' Charlotte had turned back to me and was beckoning me over. 'You remember Artie?'

I walked over to join them. Artie smiled and continued talking to Charlotte about a guy he liked.

'Oh *God*,' said Artie, 'this could be *it*, Lottie. He could be *the one*. He is so exceptionally cute.'

'Chill, Casanova, you don't even know his name.' She was teasing him, but they were both smiling.

'Who cares? I just want to know his number ...'

They carried on like that, trying to figure out if they could find this fella on Instagram from just his school uniform. Everything about this place was making me feel like some kind of alien. You'd never get a fella in our estate talking about a guy in that way. Not that there weren't any gay guys. It was just different to hear someone being so open about it.

I followed them to class feeling a bit like a puppy on a lead. Charlotte tried to include me in the conversation but there wasn't much I could say. I could hardly give Artie advice on stalking some stranger. We signed in and went to Spanish and I sat in the same seat I'd sat in the day before. The iPad was on the table, and Don Antonio looked up from his desk briefly, nodding to the table to make sure I knew it was for me. I nodded back, grateful.

He cleared his throat and the class settled immediately.

FEDERICO GARCÍA LORCA

The words appeared on the whiteboard as he typed them into his own iPad.

'You know what to do,' Don Antonio said.

The class began typing too. Words started appearing on the screen, but not his words this time. He nodded to Charlotte and gently waved a finger from her to me. She indicated the correct tab on the app.

'We have to type whatever we know about Lorca. He does this at the start of every topic,' she whispered.

I looked at the screen to see what had already been written:

> Born in 1898.
>
> Lorca lived in Granada.
>
> He wrote poems and plays.
>
> He got killed during the Spanish Civil War.

Everyone was typing away. What did I know about Lorca? He was Spanish. He wrote this poem about the moon that I hadn't translated last night. I tried to think of the book that the poem was in. It had Lorca on the front cover. He looked young and he was half smiling, looking directly at the camera. Probably a bit of a show-off, I thought. Dark hair and eyes. Good-looking. Probably a bit of a ladies' man? Sexy Spanish poet? Bound to be. I had to write something.

Lorca was fond of the women.

You could almost hear the soft taps on the iPads stop in unison. The words stopped appearing on the screen.

'Who wrote this?' Don Antonio asked, highlighting my line on the screen with a swipe of his hand.

Oh shit. Did it sound like I was being flippant? I hadn't meant to. Nobody spoke. There was no way I was going to tell him that it was me.

Silence.

Finally a half-smile crept onto Don Antonio's face and he flashed a glance at me, my face burning. He must have figured it out. 'I'm going to assume this was a genuine mistake and not a comment on Lorca's preferences.'

A couple of kids giggled. Don Antonio erased the last part of the line and typed in 'the men' where 'the women' had been. *Shit.* Why had I assumed Lorca was straight? I felt like a complete tit. I swear my face was burning so hard I was worried about setting fire to the sodding iPad. I remembered what Charlotte had said to Artie about Don Antonio: *I think you're more his type.* Oh my God. He probably thought I was a homophobe. Some little backwards dick from the estate who couldn't cope with gay people. I wanted to die.

Don Antonio was reading out the other lines that students had written, correcting them when necessary, swapping some lines around until the whole thing was a short bio of Lorca. He tapped his screen and a printer in the corner started whirring. He handed out the sheets for our folders. At Laney we'd all have had to copy the stuff off the board and it would've taken the rest of the class. As he passed me to set the sheet on my desk he put his hand flat on it and tapped once, gently. It was a thing you could've missed but I knew it meant *We're cool.* Don't ask me how I knew, I just did. Even so, as the class ended I wanted to say something. I knew that if I left the room without having explained myself I'd be wondering all day about whether or not I had *started off on the wrong foot.* The class filed out and I approached Don Antonio's desk. He looked up and smiled, taking off his glasses.

'Andrew!' His accent was half Spain, half Northern Ireland. 'How are you finding things at Cooke's?'

'Em, OK,' I said. *Weird*, I thought. *Weird and intense.*

'¡Muy bien! How can I help you?'

I cleared my throat. 'I, um, I just wanted to say that ... well, I think you know that it was me who wrote the thing about Lorca liking girls, and ...'

He leaned back on his seat. He had this amused look on his face, like he was loving every second. I suddenly needed the loo really badly. I tried to focus. He wasn't saying anything so I had to finish.

'So, I ... well, it was a mistake. But I just wanted you to know that it was a genuine mistake. I mean ... I wasn't making a joke or anything like that.'

'I know,' he said, smiling. 'It's fine, Andrew. Really. Don't worry about it.'

And that was that. I felt the tension drop away from my neck, my shoulders. 'OK, cool. Well, thanks.'

'You like poetry?' he asked.

I didn't know what to say. I knew that the answer, if anyone else had asked it, would be to shrug my shoulders, as if it didn't mean a thing to me, maybe even a slight sneer as if to say, *What's poetry and how should I know?*

But it felt wrong to lie to him, so I said yes. Because that's the truth. I do like poetry. I am a boy who likes poetry. I could feel my face burning.

'It's just poetry,' he said with another half-smile. 'Nothing to get worried about.'

I felt stupid. It was OK for him. He was a teacher – they're *allowed* to like stuff.

'OK. Thanks, sir.' I felt I had to say something to make it seem like I wasn't totally embarrassed, even though every part of me was screaming. 'I'm enjoying the class.'

God, that made it worse. I knew my face was beaming. *Please just let this conversation end.*

He nodded and smiled. 'Bueno. I will see you next time.'

I turned to walk away.

'Although,' he said. I stopped and turned around again. 'Although, really, if you want to be in my class you need to do your own work, OK?'

The homework translation. It was on his desk in front of him. He must have caught a look at it during class. I think I stopped breathing for a second. This was bad.

He gave a quiet chuckle. 'You're not in trouble, Andrew. But start well, OK? Put the work in and it will work for you.'

I nodded, shamed to the spot, unable to move.

'It's hard work at Cooke's. Not just *this* kind of work.' He lifted the homework and dropped it again on the desk. 'In fact, that might be the easiest part of being here if you're a bit of an outsider.'

I looked at the framed photo on his desk. An elderly couple sitting outdoors at a café table under an umbrella, beaming like they'd won the lottery.

'My parents,' said Don Antonio, noticing the direction of my gaze. 'In Madrid. Where I'm from.'

'Do you miss it?' I said, before realising how nosey and casual that sounded. It didn't faze him. He raised his eyebrows slightly.

'Yes. I'm from Belfast now as well, though.' The smile returned. 'Go on,' he said. 'You'll be late to whatever's next.' He waved me off. 'Do your homework!' he called as I left. There was a hint of humour to his tone but I knew he meant it. I knew that I wouldn't copy Charlotte's work again.

As I stepped out into the corridor, I went over it in my head: *Put the work in and it will work for you.*

The guy at the locker next to mine was tall and clean-looking, like someone from a boy band. He smiled and held out a hand. 'Adam Bailey.'

I shook his hand. 'Drew Kelly.'

He nodded, closing his locker. 'I know. Newbie, right?'

'Yes.'

'Sports?'

'What?'

'Sports. Do you play?'

'Em. Football, I suppose.'

'Got a team?'

This was like a frickin' police interview. 'No. Just at the weekend. With mates. You know?'

He nodded. 'Cool. Well, maybe sign up for soccer? It's not as important as rugby, but we have a good team.'

He closed his locker and patted my right arm, as if he was my dad or something, as he walked off. It was the weirdest exchange I'd ever had in my life. I took a moment to process it. Some complete stranger had introduced himself, asked me a load of questions and then told me to join the football team, even though it wasn't as important as rugby. What the hell was that all about?

I shook myself and rummaged around in my bag looking for my book for physics. When I closed the locker Charlotte's friend was standing there. She giggled, flicking her red curls over her shoulder.

'Sorry, Drew, didn't mean to scare you.'

'No worries.' I smiled at her. What was her name, though? Lily? Lara?

'Lucy,' she said, as though she could read my mind. 'Charlotte's friend, from yesterday?'

'Yes, I remember,' I said.

'Do you know where you're going OK?'

'Not exactly,' I admitted. 'Physics. That's ... downstairs?'

'Yep. I'm going to English. I'll show you.'

We walked down the stairs together. I knew I should make conversation but it was hard to know what to say. She seemed friendly, though. And less weird than the boy I'd just met.

'Do you know someone called Adam?' I said.

She stopped walking. 'Yes. Why?' She suddenly looked serious. It made me wonder briefly if Adam was a member of staff. He had presented himself with that kind of authority. *But don't be thick, Drew, he was in school uniform.*

'I dunno. I just met him.'

She continued walking, but slower, like she wanted to take her time telling me about him. 'Adam Bailey is kind of a big deal here,' she said. 'He's the Stewards president, for one thing.'

'The what?'

'Hmmm. This might take a while to explain. Do you want to meet up at lunchtime and I'll fill you in?'

'OK.'

I had kind of been hoping to bump into Charlotte at lunchtime, but I wanted to know more about Adam. And maybe Charlotte would be there anyway. We were at the physics lab.

'This is you,' Lucy said. 'Enjoy your equations!'

'Heh. Thanks. Enjoy your ... Yeats?'

'Heaney,' she said. 'And don't worry about Adam. He's full of himself, but if you stay on the right side of him he's OK.'

I hadn't been worried about him, but I didn't find her words very comforting. I decided that I would probably be making an effort to be careful about anyone who I was meant to 'stay on the right side of'.

7. Charlotte

Lunchtime. Three messages. One from Artie going on about the *love of his life* again. It would be someone else next month. He was an incurable romantic. Last Valentine's day he had filled the sixth-form library with dried rose petals, each with Luke Miller's name written in Sharpie on it. The sixth-form librarian, Ms Smyth, wasn't impressed. But it did the trick. He and Luke were together for a month after the rose-petal thing until Artie finally got sick of how intense Luke was being, phoning him all the time, always wanting to go out. Incurable romantic – no sense of irony. I smiled at his message – a detailed checklist of the various perfections of his new object of affection:

> Dark blue eyes, so unique, they're almost purple, OMG he's probably the reincarnation of Prince; jet black shoulder length hair that looks like he's permanently standing on the edge of a cliff in a music video; you can see the muscles in his thighs when he's sitting on the bus in his skinny jeans …

On and on it went.

There was another message from Mum, about not forgetting to put the chicken on to roast when I got home. And the last message was from Adam. I left it unread. I hadn't had a WhatsApp from him in weeks and whatever it was I didn't want to know. I considered blocking him, but I knew that it would be a mistake. You don't just block Adam Bailey.

I put my phone face down on the table as Lucy and Drew sat down. I was glad they'd arrived together. I liked Drew. I thought he'd probably fit in with our group pretty well. It wasn't easy for newbies at Cooke's. The sixth form was already a culture shock for people who had been going here since prep. God knows what it was like for a kid from his estate.

'Hiya!' I said as they sat down.

'Hey gurl,' said Lucy.

'Hi,' said Drew.

'How's your day going?' I asked him.

'All right. The Spanish teacher knew I'd copied your work.'

Shit! That wasn't good. He'd probably have guessed it was my idea.

'Don't worry,' he said, probably noticing the panic on my face. 'It's cool. It won't happen again, and I'm sorry I put you in that position.'

Cute smile, I thought.

'You didn't. I offered,' I said, trying to sound like it wasn't a big deal. If my mum found out she'd totally flip.

'I know. But ... it's a big change for me coming here. I have to start taking responsibility. Putting the work in.'

It sounded like a rehearsed speech, or a mantra.

'Cool. Well, if you need any help, short of plagiarism I mean, then you can ask me. Or any of us, really.'

I looked at Lucy, who nodded in agreement. Drew smiled awkwardly and thanked us. I looked at the phone lying face down on the table, begging me to either turn it over and look at that message or throw it in the bin. It was hard to imagine which would be the worse option. I wouldn't think about it now.

'So,' said Lucy, a hint of excitement in her eyes. I was relieved. A bit of gossip was just what I needed.

'Spill,' I said.

'Drew has met Adam.'

For God's sake. There was no escape from him. Lucy was grinning as if I'd want nothing more than to spend the rest of lunchtime talking about Adam Bailey. Urgh. I contemplated faking an urgent text that would call me away. But I knew I couldn't do that or I was going to spend all year running away from him. *Breathe, Charlotte. Get a grip.*

'Oh,' I said, trying to sound unbothered. 'And what did you think of him?' I asked Drew.

Drew shrugged. 'He wanted me to sign up for football or something. Seemed a bit obsessed with sports.'

'Welcome to Cooke's,' I said.

'It's a Stewards thing,' said Lucy.

'You said that before,' said Drew, taking a slug of his Coke. 'So Stewards. What are they?'

'A bunch of knobheads,' I said, as Lucy opened her mouth to explain.

She giggled. 'Maybe so,' she said, 'but they're powerful knobheads.'

She was right – they were powerful. You try breaking up with someone like that. Nobody knows what to say. You break up with anyone else – a normal person, even a popular normal person – and your girl-friends will stick with you, his guy-friends will stick with him. You will text your girl-friends saying things like *I hate him! But I still love him!* and they'll text back things like *He isn't worth it. His breath smells and when he's forty he's gonna have a beer belly like his dad and you'll still be hot and married to Harry Styles.* But split up with Adam Bailey and the world on your end goes quiet. You'll get *I'm so sorry you split up* and *You must be devastated*, but that's it. None of your girl-friends would dare to piss off a Steward. They know better. Everyone does. Well, with the exception of Artie, who is the only person I know who truly does not care what anyone thinks of him.

I watched Lucy animatedly filling Drew in about the Stewards – their rules, their traditions, their promises. He was wide-eyed.

'So, basically,' Drew said, 'if I become friends with Adam I'll have a better chance at the scholarship?'

'Definitely,' said Lucy.

Drew went quiet then, but I was sure he was desperately plotting ways to get on the good side of some sports hero that he didn't know and didn't have anything in common with. His food was still sitting on the tray, untouched, when the bell went.

He left with Lucy, who was still chattering away. I meant to head straight to the library but instead I went to the toilet block and locked myself in a cubicle. I took out my phone and stared at the notification icon for a while, my finger hovering over the little dustbin symbol. And then I clicked on the message from Adam. I had thought it would be some passive-aggressive note, maybe an attempt at friendship. Adam hated to be disliked. And he knew I didn't like him. Our break-up hadn't been one of those 'It's not you, it's me' break-ups. It had been quick and deliberate, over within seconds, something which had been coming for a while, and when I did it I knew that it was the right thing to do. I felt immediately relieved to be rid of him. And now here I was, hiding in the toilets and staring at a message which was letting me know that I would never, ever be rid of him.

It was a video. The attached message said *Miss me?* I watched a couple of seconds of it before realising what it was. It was us. Me and Adam. Together on his bed. I hadn't known he'd filmed us. He'd never said.

A thousand thoughts were racing through my head and all of them began with *NO*. My heart was pounding and I started to breathe more heavily and soon it was becoming hard to breathe at all and, as I struggled to let the message to *calm down* override the voices in my mind, I started to choke. Then I was on my knees on the toilet floor, vomiting into the bowl, my brain screaming so hard that I wondered if anyone outside the cubicle would be able to hear it. I grabbed the toilet-roll dispenser and forced myself back up onto the seat, holding my head and searching for a good thought, one that would make everything OK again. How many other people had seen it? Why was he sending it now? What was the point? Why was he doing this? What did he want? What was I meant to say or do? Should I tell someone? Who?

There was a gentle knock on the cubicle door.

'Hello?' the voice said. 'Are you OK in there?'

It wasn't a voice I recognised.

'I'm fine,' I choked out. My own voice sounded nothing like me.

'I heard you being sick. Do you need some help?'

I wanted to laugh. It actually seemed hilarious for some reason. Did I need some help? My life was over.

I thought about Lucy laughing with Drew, just a few minutes ago. They seemed so far away now. It was like that message had flung me right back into the middle of last year when everything was about Adam, when I was so in love with Adam, and then I was in his world completely, and soon I realised that in his world there's only really room for Adam and the things that he wants, and then I was breaking up with him and I was free again and the future looked bright. I had been so stupid to think that I could just leave him.

'I'm really OK,' I said, trying not to gag again, willing them to go away.

'OK. Well ... I'm going now but I'll call back in a few minutes to make sure you're all right.'

'OK. Thanks.'

They left and I threw up again, the acid burning my throat, until there was nothing left and I was retching and trying to breathe normally. I knew I had to leave before the Concerned Student came back, but where could I go? What if I bumped into Adam? My phone buzzed and I physically jumped. But it was only Artie.

> In study. So boooooored. Where are you?
>
> I thought you had study this period?

My whole body was shaking but I made myself text him:

> Want to get out of here?
>
> I really need a coffee.

He replied:

> Oh hell yes. See you at Buster's?

Buster's was just across the street but a world apart from this place, and now that we were in sixth form, we were allowed to go there for coffee during free periods. Adam wouldn't be seen dead in a place like Buster's.

See you there.

Artie was just what I needed right now. A friend who would listen when I wanted him to but who would happily fill the gaps with his own chatter when I needed to focus on something apart from myself. I needed that much more than I needed a coffee.

8. Drew

Put the work in and it will work for you. I wrote it on a scrap of paper before the teacher turned up. He hadn't been talking about the Stewards, but it applied all the same. What kind of work did I need to do? How honest could I be? I thought about the poem about the moon – the impenetrable paths. All of this was going to be harder than I'd imagined.

9. Charlotte

Buster's Books and Coffee was dark. Always. It didn't matter if the sun was blazing outside; as soon as you walked through that door you might as well have been underground. Only the upper school was allowed to leave during lunch or free periods, so it was quiet during the day, with only the occasional student coming in to take a coffee break or study in a less well-lit environment. The café was L-shaped with a small stage at the apex of the L and a counter with Portia's home-made cakes and a till at the side. They only did cakes and coffee, sometimes soup if Portia had had time to make it the night before. The walls were uneven and whitewashed, but you could hardly see the white because they were covered in posters advertising poetry events and performance nights, people's sketches of Portia and the odd framed painting that customers had done for her. None of the cups and saucers matched and the tables were old and wonky.

Artie was already there by the time I arrived. He was engrossed in one of Portia's books. It was *Valley of the Dolls*. I hoped he was loving it so much that he'd spend the rest of the afternoon telling me all about it.

'Hey,' I said, slumping into the chair opposite him. He jumped slightly and the table lurched, spilling his coffee into the too-big saucer. He grinned.

'Hiya!' he said, leaving the book face down on the table before pouring the coffee from the saucer back into his cup. I fumbled around with a napkin, rolling it up to perform the necessary DIY job on the table leg.

'How's the book?' I said.

'Amazing!' he said. 'I think Portia deliberately leaves it out for me now. Anyway. How are you?'

Awful. Crap. Horrendous.

I thought back to the video from Adam. None of those words could fully sum it up. I briefly considered telling Artie. But it would have been a bad idea. He was a great person, but there's no way he would have kept it to himself.

'Hey,' he said more softly. 'Are you OK?'

My eyes filled up. So much for keeping this thing to myself.

'You're not OK,' he said.

He touched my hand and I pulled it away, not because I didn't want him to, but because I needed to pull myself together. Immediately.

'I'm fine. Really.' I sniffed and dabbed my face where the tears had spilled over slightly. 'It's PMS. There's literally nothing wrong.'

He frowned. I knew he didn't believe me.

'Wait there,' he said as he left the table.

By the time he had returned with a large mug of coffee and a huge slice of Portia's chocolate cake, I had managed to regain my composure, or at least pretend to.

'You're the best, Artie,' I said, smiling at him. He smiled back.

'I won't pry,' he said, 'but if there's anything you want to talk about ...'

'I know. Thanks. I'm really OK.'

He nodded.

'What I really need,' I continued, 'Is to talk about some-thing other than school. Anything at all. Your book. Or what's on TV. Or this guy you've been chasing.'

Artie's eyes lit up at the mention of him. He sighed deeply. 'He really is the perfect man, Lottie. Apparently he's the singer in a band as well. I bet he's brilliant. What do you think? Should I ask him out?'

'I don't know.'

'What?' He sat up, outraged. 'Why shouldn't I ask him out? Do you think he'd say no? Why?!'

I laughed. 'Calm down. I'm sure he'd jump at the chance. Who wouldn't?' Artie smiled again. 'I just meant I don't know him so how would I know if he's good enough for my best gay boy-friend?'

'Your best gay boy-friend? Do you have another gay boy-friend? Who is he? I'll fight him ...'

I loved it when Artie was in a playful mood. It was ex-actly what I'd been hoping for. We chatted for another half hour, him going on about whether or not to ask out the guy he liked, and me trying not to choke on the chocolate cake as he made me snort with laughter. It was almost time to go back to class when Portia came over to say hello.

Portia was someone you might think of as elderly if you saw her in the street: grey hair in a bob, and she wasn't really short but she always leaned slightly forward so she looked shorter than she was. And she moved slowly, but it was like she was just being deliberate about it, as if she was always thinking about every step and she had all the time in the world. She had a casual way about her that reminded me of someone moving around their own living room, fixing cushions or admiring pictures in frames.

'Here. Have yous seen this?' She lifted a flyer from another table and dropped it in front of us. 'Might be up your street. Anyway, finished with these cups?' She lifted the empties and walked off.

The leaflet had the words POETRY SLAM in all caps at the top of the page. And underneath: OPENING NIGHT SATURDAY 6th OCTOBER BUSTER'S BOOKS AND COFFEE. Then there was an Instagram link. In the centre of the flyer was a picture of the head and shoulders of a drag queen. She had sparkling silver eyelashes and the rest of her make-up was just as dramatic – a swoop of electric blue over her winking eye and brightly glittering red lips in an audacious open mouth. Her hair was gigantic. At the bottom of the page it said COMPÈRE: MS JEWEL NATIONALITY.

Artie looked at me open-mouthed.

'No,' I said, knowing exactly what he was thinking.

He pouted. 'Come on, Lottie. This is totally what you need. You've wanted to do this for ages!'

I shook my head, but it was true. I had thought about reading poetry in public for a while. I'd seen people do it in Buster's the odd time. We watched YouTube videos of spoken-word poets at poetry club. I liked the idea that you could stand up in front of a crowd of strangers and tell them what you were thinking. It was different to anything else. It wasn't like busking because it was just you and the words. And it wasn't like the debating society – it was much less formal than that, more personal. I admired the people who did it. But I'd never have the guts. And besides ...

'Mum would never let me,' I said.

'What? Come on, Lottie. You're seventeen. She wouldn't have to know about it.'

'Yeah, but if she found out ... Can you imagine her reaction if she knew I was hanging out with Ms Jewel Nationality?' I held the picture in front of Artie's face.

He got up. It was time for us to leave.

'You know you want to,' he said as he pushed in his chair.

'I really don't,' I replied.

It was only half true, though. I wanted to be the kind of person who would do something like that. I wished I was bolder, like Artie. I pushed my chair in too, and we walked back to school. On the way in I caught sight of Adam as he walked past the entrance on his way to the sports field, rugby ball hugged tightly underneath his arm. He smirked at me and it was like the past hour hadn't even happened – the wave of nausea flooded all the thoughts about Artie and the poetry slam and I knew as I gripped my files close to my chest that I'd never be rid of him.

10. Drew

She was nice, Lucy. But she wasn't hot like Charlotte. I mean, don't get me wrong, she wasn't bad-looking. Definitely cute. Amazing hair. But Charlotte had something about her, something in how she looked when she was concentrating really hard on an essay, when she didn't realise anyone was looking at her. Whatever it was it was hard not to think about. I was trying, though. I wrote it in my notebook: *Put the work in and it'll work for you.* And then I tore up the page, feeling like an idiot, imagining what someone like Dale or Jonny would think if they could see me trying to embed some worthy inspirational quote in my head so that I could do my homework instead of thinking about the sexiest girl in the sixth form. I wrote it down again, this time in Spanish: *Aplícate, y el trabajo te ayuda.*

I'm not thick – I know that loads of people in the world speak Spanish. But I was pretty certain that nobody on this estate could. And that made it a secret language, like Dothraki or Klingon. Not that anyone from Greenwood was climbing through my bedroom window to read my notebook. But somehow I felt like I was free if I could write in Spanish. Like even if the notebook grew legs and flung itself out into the street and shouted READ ME to the passing kids who then copied the words all over the walls of the houses, I'd still be safe. I could be completely myself in Spanish. I could write poems about sex and feeling lonely and feeling angry and it was all cool, nobody would ever know. *Aplícate, y el trabajo te ayuda.* That's what I needed for now, though: focus.

I went to the kitchen to get a can of Boost and chugged it as I stood next to the fridge. As the caffeine buzzed in my head it all felt more clear. I'd think about it like homework. Up to now I'd been coasting – just doing whatever was next; I'd got a paper round cos Dale's uncle offered it to me, and I used the money for smokes because that's what everyone did; I stayed in school because there was nothing better to do; I passed my exams because I could. Just going with the flow. You could kind of guess where everyone would end up because it was usually what their parents did. Although, funny enough, it wasn't me that surprised everyone, it was Dale, failing his GCSEs and then deciding that instead of just signing on he wanted to be a mechanic and to get a car. It sounds wrong to be surprised about it, but everyone was. There was a teacher in school who called Dale a waster one time. Everyone hated him. That was the sort of thing he'd just casually say to kids: 'You're lazy and you'll never do anything.' He thought he was class because he was from Greenwood too and he'd gone to university. He was a twat, but the thing was that nobody really thought he was wrong about Dale. And then after Dale left school he just started being different. It was like he grew up overnight and became this actual adult, wanting to study and get a job. Sometimes you had to go after stuff – make things happen.

I crumpled the can and chucked it in the bin.

'That stuff gave Davey Lennard a heart attack you know,' said Mum bustling into the room with a big pile of washing.

Davey Lennard: homeless alcoholic. Widely known to have been huffing glue on the daily. Found dead in the rec last Christmas. But according to my mum it was the caffeine that killed him.

I ignored her and ran upstairs to my room and opened a page of my notebook, writing in Spanish:

> *Things to solve:*
> I fancy Charlotte.
> I need to get in with Adam somehow.
> I have to do this bloody essay.
>
> *Things to do:*
> Text Charlotte. Just to say hi. Be cool.
> Sign up for football.
> Just write the bloody essay.

I decided I'd text Charlotte after the essay. I opened the textbook again. Somehow writing the list had made some space in my head for the Spanish Civil War, and a couple of hours later it was dark outside and everyone in my essay was dead, Franco was in charge and, thank God, I'd finished it.

Maybe I was on a high because I'd managed to complete the work, or maybe the caffeine was still in my system; either way I was feeling really good. I lifted my phone. Seventeen notifications, mostly from the estate group chat talking nonsense about some kid who might be going to get a kicking for selling weed. Two texts. Both from Lucy.

> Hey Drew. Probably barking up the wrong tree entirely, but if you want to join poetry

group it's starting tomorrow at lunchtime in
our English room.

Then, ten minutes later, another text.

It's a good laugh.
And it's OK if you're a beginner.
And we do cool trips and stuff.
LOL sorry if this is weird because you totally
hate poetry.

It made me smile, how keen she was. I wondered if I
could do the double-life thing – be a geeky poetry kid in
school and, at home, the type of person who would piss
themselves laughing if they found out a person like me
was a geeky poetry kid. I'd play it safe for now. I texted
Lucy back:

Thanks Lucy.
I'm signing up for football tomorrow
so will give it a miss as I might need to find
the sign-up sheet.
Hard to keep up with all the homework!

I lay back on the bed, feeling clever, keeping my op-
tions open. I was totally in control here. She texted back
straight away:

No problem!
Good idea to sign up for soccer.
Adam will be impressed!
Let me know if you need any help
with the homework.
L x

I grinned to myself. She liked me. I was eighty per cent sure of it. I looked up Charlotte's number and began to write a text to her.

Hi Charlotte. Drew here.

Hmmm. I needed a reason to contact her. I couldn't just write *Hi Charlotte. Drew here. I can't stop thinking about how great you smell.* How about ...

Hi Charlotte.
Drew here.
It was just the essay for Don Antonio
tomorrow, wasn't it?
I can't remember if we had vocab as well.
Sent

I waited on the bed for five minutes, expecting that she might text right back the way that Lucy did, but no luck. Maybe she was in the middle of the essay or something. I went downstairs. Mum was sitting on the armchair, sleeping, Dad reading the paper on the sofa with a can of lager balancing on the armrest. I sat down beside him. He didn't look up or anything, but he moved across slightly so I could have some space.

'All right, son?' he said, as though he could read the paper and chat at the same time.

'Yeah.'

I flicked through the channels with the telly on mute so as not to wake up Mum, finally settling on some nature thing which you could watch with no sound – a lion slowly stalking a gazelle and then starting to run towards it.

'School going OK?' said Dad, still not looking up.

'Yep.'

'Homework?'

'Loads.'

'Girls?'

'What?' I looked at him.

He smirked from behind his paper. 'Girls, son. All work and no play, you know?'

God. I was not having this conversation with my dad. He'd never asked me about stuff like this. There were definite lines in our house. Don't get me wrong, my parents were dead on. But there were lines that you didn't cross. And talking to me about girls and stuff – that was one of them. I was not up for going there. I focused on the lion, now chewing happily on gazelle-leg. My phone buzzed. Charlotte.

Just the essay.

That was it. The whole message. My immediate response was to panic. Was she pissed off with me? Then I caught myself on. Maybe she was just busy or tired. I checked the clock – 10.30 p.m. I was tired too. That must've been it.

'I'm going to sign up for football tomorrow,' I said.

Dad put down the paper and looked at me.

'Are you?' he said. His tone was soft.

'Yeah.'

I thought about telling him about Adam and the scholarship and how Lucy had told me that Adam and his group basically controlled who would get it. Dad was off on one, though. Talking about his childhood and playing football for his school and how someone from the Glens came out to watch them one time and offered Dad a chance to try out for the junior team.

'Had to go and work in them days, though,' he said with a sigh. 'It was off down the shipyard with my da. No time for dreaming about football. I'm proud of you, son.'

That threw me a bit. I'd thought it was a safe enough topic, and suddenly here he was getting misty-eyed. Jesus.

'It's only football, Da.'

He smiled gently. 'It's not only anything,' he said. 'You're making something of yourself.'

He gave me a pat on the leg as he got up and stretched. He went over to Mum and started to wake her up to come up to bed. It would all work out, I thought. Everything was coming together.

11. Charlotte

'What's the meaning of *telluric*? Anyone know?'

I knew but I didn't raise my hand. I just wanted to get through the lesson and get home.

'*Telluric*, miss,' said Lucy, 'something to do with the land?'

'That's right! So which Heaney poems do you think best exemplify his *telluric* spirit? Charlotte?'

I looked up in a daze. 'Uh ... "Digging"?'

'Bingo. Twenty points to team Lucy and Charlotte!'

A couple of clicks on her computer and the text of Heaney's 'Digging' appeared on the whiteboard screen.

'Someone tell me about this poem. You all read it last night – what did you think? Come on, guys ...' She circled her hand in the air. 'Only forty minutes to go – one last push for your friendly English teacher?'

Nobody laughed, but most people smiled. Everyone liked Miss Robinson. People started calling out their ideas about the poem.

'It's literally about digging?'

'Yeah but it's also about writing.'

'It's about old age.'

'It's about self-actualisation.'

Miss Robinson made an 'oooh!' face. 'That's interesting, Mark. Can you say more about that?'

Mark looked sheepish. He couldn't help being that smart, but you could tell he hated the attention. His voice grew softer. 'Well, it's like – his dad's identity was all bound up in being a farmer, but Heaney finds himself in writing. You can see it in "Personal Helicon" too – *I rhyme to see myself*. It's like if he doesn't do poetry he'd lose himself a bit, you know? As if when he writes he feels totally OK about himself.'

Miss Robinson was nodding; other students were making notes. I was thinking about the poetry slam and wondering what it would be like to feel totally OK about yourself. Lucky Heaney. My mind drifted towards the little stage in Buster's. I imagined myself standing there and feeling totally OK in the moment. It was useless. What would I even write for a poetry slam? I wrote the word on a piece of file paper. Miss Robinson was talking about metaphors. *Slam.* My head was pounding. *Slam.* I hated him I hated him I hated him.

> Slam
>
> Slam
>
> My head against the desk
>
> Slam
>
> My heart against your knife
>
> Slam
>
> My image on your screen
>
> Slam
>
> The door on last year
>
> Slam
>
> Slam
>
> It will not close
>
> Slam

Your face in my head
Your face in my head
Your face in my head
Slam.
Slam.
Slam.

12. Drew

Charlotte wasn't there on the way to school. I had a momentary flash of anxiety wondering about the shortness of the text. But the thought was quickly replaced by the voice of Dale in my head laughing at me for getting wound up about a girl. I grinned to myself. He was right. I hardly knew Charlotte. I mean, who cared if she'd taken offence to something I'd said or done? Anyway, there was always Lucy. Maybe I should concentrate on her. I was walking up the street towards the supermarket, trying to dodge the dog poo and listing Lucy's best features in my head, starting with her long legs in those navy sheer tights, when I heard a voice behind me.

''Bout ye?'

I turned around and holy hell if it wasn't Karen. I hadn't seen her since we'd broken up. And she looked great. I mean, she was only wearing her Tesco uniform, but her hair looked shiny and soft and she still had that sparkle.

'Oh. Hiya,' I said, immediately feeling about five years old in my school uniform with my bag of books.

She grinned. 'I take it you've heard?'

I hadn't meant to stare at her belly. 'Em. Yeah. Congratulations.'

'Thanks.'

It was hard to know what to say after that. We walked on in silence for a bit. Tesco was five minutes away. I searched my brain for something to say other than 'WTF,

Karen? We were broken up for, like, ten seconds, and now you're up the duff?'

Eventually she broke the silence.

'I hope it's not too weird for you,' she said.

'What? Oh, no way. I mean, I think it's great!' *Slightly overcompensating there, Drew.*

'Oh. Well, good. Because I'd really like you to come to the wedding.'

'What?' I stopped dead in my tracks. She couldn't mean she was getting married to Jonny. We had literally just broken up!

Her face became serious and I thought I could feel a sight tone of sympathy in her voice.

'Jonny and me. We're getting married. We just ... we thought it was the right thing, you know?'

I did know. It's what people did sometimes. It's what my parents did.

'But you don't have to do that these days,' I said. 'I mean, nobody minds if a baby's parents aren't married.'

Karen's face darkened. '*I* mind,' she said.

I knew by her tone that I couldn't say anything else. It was none of my business. And why did I care anyway? We were nearly at Tesco and she brightened up again.

'Anyway,' she said, 'hopefully you'll come. You can bring someone, obviously. A girlfriend. Or whatever.' She was trying to be nice, and mature, but it was weird having this conversation and I was glad it was about to end. 'See you later then?'

I nodded. 'Yeah. See you, Karen.'

I walked the rest of the way to school in a daze. Ten minutes ago I'd been worrying about which girl to fancy more in school. Now I was thinking about my ex-girlfriend who was going to be married with a baby this time next year. If we'd stayed together maybe it would have been my baby, my wedding. The thought should have horrified me, but it didn't. I just felt a bit sad, like I was walking off in the opposite direction – not just right now, but in life generally; away from Karen, away from Greenwood. By the time I got to Cooke's I hated myself in my stupid childish uniform and I hated all the other kids smiling at one another, and chatting about stupid childish gossip, and worrying about their homework the way I'd been worrying about it the night before. I didn't love Karen, for God's sake. Maybe I just didn't want her to be happy with anyone else. *Nice one, Drew. What a guy!*

I shook myself out of it and looked at my phone: 8.50 a.m. Time to spare. I headed down the stairs to the boys' PE rooms and found the noticeboard. Sign-up sheets for various sports clubs were almost full. One space left on the football list. I stuck my hand in my bag, looking for a pen, and then one appeared in front of my face. I turned around.

'Good choice,' said Adam.

I smiled, glad that he was noticing. I took the silver pen from him and wrote my name up. Practice would start next week after school. I'd have to find the proper kit from somewhere but I'd think about that later.

'Heading to the form room?' he said. He didn't wait for me to answer. 'I'll walk with you.'

It was some distance away, and as we walked Adam started talking. It was easy being with him: he led everything. He led us to the cafeteria because he wanted to get a coffee; he led us to the economics room because he needed to leave a paper in; he led the conversation, which was mostly about sports. He was so confident. When we were almost at the form room we stopped at our lockers. Charlotte walked past.

'Hiya!' I said.

She looked at us blankly and she didn't speak back. Well, that was it, I was forgetting about her. She clearly wasn't interested.

'Moody,' I said, making a face at Adam.

He sighed. 'That's women for you. Can't live with them, can't shag without them.'

He winked and I laughed even though it was a nasty joke. Charlotte had looked terrible. I mean, I had decided not to care about her, but I couldn't help wondering if she was ill or something. Adam shut his locker and spun the padlock code.

'Let's talk about the Stewards,' he said. 'Lunchtime today?'

I thought about Lucy's text about poetry club. There was no way I was going to tell Adam of all people that that's what I'd rather be doing.

'Yeah, sure!'

He nodded and headed off to his form room without saying anything else. We hadn't even arranged where to meet but I assumed that he'd find me. I wondered what it was about. Maybe some information about applying for the scholarship? I hoped so. Whatever the reason, it was clear that he was cool with me hanging out with him at lunchtime and that could only be a good thing. I was doing it – putting the work in and letting it work for me.

13. Charlotte

I still hadn't deleted it. For some reason it felt like if I had that video on my phone then nobody else could have it – even though I knew he had it on his phone and could send it to anyone he liked. The worst thing was wondering why he'd sent it to me. Was he just being cruel? Or was it a threat? If it was a threat then what did he want from me? Maybe he was just letting me know, in case he wanted something in the future. That would be like him, but I couldn't ask.

I couldn't tell anyone else either. I knew I wasn't the only person in sixth form to have slept with their boyfriend. Artie had done it, and Nick and Anna were practically married, but I had never told anyone that I'd slept with Adam. It was private. And we'd only done it twice before we broke up. I'd almost told Lucy but she had started going on about how glad she was that she wasn't the only virgin in the class and so I didn't say anything because I had broken up with Adam by then and, to be honest, I wished I hadn't done it with him, so I suppose I had been pretending to myself that I hadn't. And now I had this evidence in my pocket. Lucy would hate me for lying to her. Artie might side with her. Everyone would think I was a slut for filming it, even though I hadn't known he'd had a camera.

I couldn't stop thinking about it. I couldn't eat. Mum had raised an eyebrow at breakfast when I left my eggs on the plate.

'You're not going anorexic, are you, Charlotte?'

'What? No, of course not!'

'It's not like you to leave breakfast.'

'I'm not feeling the best. It's my period.'

'You do look a bit pale,' Mum said, frowning.

'I'm fine,' I said. 'See you later.'

It was all I could choke out before grabbing my stuff and running out the door. One of the advantages of having a busy mum was at least she couldn't spend the morning wondering if I was OK.

I got to the English room for poetry club at the same time as Lucy. Artie was already there with a handful of other students. He had the MS JEWEL NATIONALITY flyer for the poetry slam on the table and the other students were looking at it and giggling. He wasn't going to let it lie.

I sat down with the others and Artie banged his cup on the table. 'Order, ladies and, well, ladies. I hereby declare this year's poetry club open for business!'

I couldn't help but smile as the small group applauded itself. This was a familiar space. It was a small group and we only sometimes wrote poems, but when we did we read them out loud. Lucy produced a packet of biscuits and the younger students started grabbing them.

'Oi! Leave some for the elders,' said Artie.

We talked about the poetry slam and, although Artie didn't mention me, he kept looking at me, and I knew what he was thinking.

'I'd so love to go,' said Emma, one of the younger students, 'but I'm not even allowed to watch *Ru Paul's Drag Race*. There's no way I'd be allowed to see an actual drag queen. Are you going?' She looked at Artie.

'Absolutely. And Lucy and Charlotte. Aren't we?'

'I can't wait!' Lucy beamed.

'Awwwk. Will you take a video for us?' said Emma.

'Of course!' said Artie with a smile.

'Hey,' said Lucy to me, 'I wonder if Drew would like to go?'

'Why don't you ask him?' I said.

Lucy went pink and didn't reply. *Wow*, I thought, *she really does like him*. Lucy had mentioned him a couple of times already today and I knew that she'd invited him to the poetry group. I could see the attraction. Drew was definitely cute. He had this kind of lopsided smile that lit up his eyes, and great hair – thick and black and slightly too long and unruly for a Cooke's boy. But I knew that the reason he wasn't at poetry club was that he was hanging out with Adam, and for that reason I had decided to keep my distance. Lucy was welcome to him. I only hoped that Adam wouldn't turn him into a Steward clone.

'Hey, anyway,' I said, shaking myself out of the anxious spiral I was getting into, 'I found this great Kae Tempest poem on YouTube today. Here, look ...'

I fumbled with my phone and played the video for the group. For the rest of lunchtime everyone shared YouTube poetry videos and ate biscuits and talked about the slam, and for a few minutes I felt safe. As the bell rang my phone buzzed and my heart lurched. It was only Mum but the sound was enough of a reminder that I wasn't safe, that I couldn't ever be safe now.

We filed out and Artie slipped his arm through mine. 'Cheer up, hun. It's only triple history.'

I wished it was only triple history.

14. Drew

The house was freezing. I'd put my hoody on over my school jumper but my hands were still cold as I tried to write. Well, that's what I told myself – *I can't concentrate, can I? Because: cold hands.*

For the millionth time since I'd started at Cooke's I thought about Dale and Karen and everyone from Greenwood. Only a few months ago we were at school together, none of us ever doing homework, hanging out at the rec, the lads kicking the ball round, the girls complaining that all we were interested in was football, while they stood on the sidelines in high heels, goosepimples popping on their bare legs. Eventually we'd stop and head down to McDonald's.

'Four medium chips and a large Diet Coke.'

'It's fries,' Karen would say.

'We're not in New York, are we? It's not as if they'll not know what chips are.'

She'd roll her eyes like I was a little kid, but once we got the chips I'd stick one in either side of my mouth like fangs and make her laugh. She always had notions, Karen. When I went to her house I'd catch her gazing at Kim Kardashian in a magazine.

'You fancy her or something?'

She'd throw the magazine at me. 'Shut up!'

I knew she was dreaming about being that rich, that popular. We all were, but nobody would ever say it out loud. I still could hardly believe it. How was she my girlfriend a year ago and now engaged to someone else and having their baby?

I blinked hard and tried to concentrate on the books. The pen had left a dent in my finger I'd been gripping it so hard. *What can you find out about the influence of societal tensions leading up to the Spanish Civil War on Lorca's writing?* Nothing. I couldn't find out anything because, to be honest, I couldn't even be bothered to Google it.

But I also didn't want to sit there thinking about last year and how I never saw my friends from Greenwood any more. It had only been a few weeks since I started school but it felt like ages. I missed them and I wished I didn't have to do rubbish things like join a posh boys' club called the Stewards to have a chance of getting anywhere in life. Adam was OK, I thought. I mean, he wasn't from my world, but he seemed all right. I didn't care about the stuff he cared about, except for girls, but I didn't really mind listening to him go on and on about rugby fixtures and old matches, team points and sports careers. It was boring, but easy. Since the first lunch meeting I'd sat with him most days. It was an easy way to avoid Charlotte, and he seemed to like me. If we saw each other in the queue he bought me lunch. And then, finally, he invited me to join his club. A 'society' he called it.

'It's an elite society,' he said in a low tone, as if it was an actual secret.

I took a bite of my burger. I'd ordered chips and a salad as well, since he was paying.

'Well, em, thanks for letting me in,' I said, mouth still full.

He smirked. 'I think you're Steward material. And what I say goes.'

He was a bit of a prick in that way. A bit up himself. But it wasn't a crime. Loads of the people at Cooke's were like that.

I nodded. The burger was really good. Miles better than you get in McDonald's. 'So, what do I have to do? To be in the club, I mean *society*, then?'

He shrugged, as if he hadn't ever thought about it. 'Nothing much. Hang with us, lend us the benefit of your worldly wisdom.'

I had no idea what that meant. Maybe he just wanted someone from my estate to prove something.

'Turn up to sports,' he continued. 'Do your homework. Ace your exams. Make us look good, basically. And just enjoy it. There are a number of *benefits* to being a Steward.'

'Benefits?' I said. 'Like what?'

'Like, the teachers go easier on you. They'll let you off with the odd missed homework as long as your grades are OK.'

'Seriously?'

He chuckled. 'Yeah, sure.' He was so casual about it. 'Don't look so confused – you'll see how it works in time. More importantly, you'll find that the ladies will take a keen interest once you start wearing this.'

He put a hand into his inside pocket and pulled out a smooth round pin. It was burgundy with a gold edge and a gold letter S in the centre. He held it out.

'Wear it with pride and with care,' he said, looking me dead in the eyes, like it was some kind of sacred seal.

'Thanks,' I said. I pinned it to my blazer.

Adam grinned widely. 'There you are,' he said. 'Welcome to the Stewards! Now, watch out for the women!'

I laughed.

'I'm serious,' he said. 'They'll be all over you before the end of the day. But, um, one thing.'

'Yeah?'

'Charlotte.'

I froze for a second – the burger midway to my mouth. Had he noticed that I liked her? How?

He took a deep breath and his face grew serious, his tone low again. 'We were ... involved. Recently.'

'Oh. I ... I didn't know.'

'Yes.' He leaned back on his chair, stretching out as if he was remembering something painful. 'We broke up.'

'Oh, I'm sorry ...'

'Hmmm. Well, anyway. She, eh, might not be ready to start seeing anyone again in the near future. Know what I mean?'

Yeah, I knew what he meant. He meant *Stay away from Charlotte or I'll mash you*. He didn't need to say anything else.

'Oh, yes. Well, no problem. I mean ... Actually, I think Lucy likes me.'

Suddenly his face changed again and he sat up straight. His eyes twinkled like a kid who's just seen Santa. 'Lucy! Well now. You dawg!'

He laughed and I laughed too, pleased that the subject had shifted slightly.

He whistled. 'Lucy Campbell. She's ... well, she's great! *Great* legs.'

It made me shudder slightly. It wasn't as if Dale and I didn't talk about girls, but it was how he'd said it. It sounded like he was talking about a cow or something.

I faked more laughter but I was glad when the bell rang and it was time to go to class. He sent me off with a clap on the back and that was that. I walked out into the corridor a new man: a Steward.

15. Charlotte

Artie was so excited, he couldn't stand still. 'Come on. Come *on*,' he said, hopping from foot to foot.

'Calm down,' I said to him. 'They're opening up now, look.'

Portia was unlocking the door and letting people into Buster's Books and Coffee for the opening night of the poetry slam. We were halfway down the queue and, to be fair, it was cold, but Artie was bursting to get in.

I might have felt excited about the evening myself if it hadn't been for what had happened earlier. A notification, in the middle of my Heaney essay. I had re-read the last stanza of 'Personal Helicon' approximately twelve times when the phone buzzed. I almost hadn't looked at it. I felt like my brain was on the tip of something. It buzzed again and I lost the thread of my thought. I was already annoyed before I saw the name. My stomach clenched. It had been a few weeks. I had almost been able to stop thinking about Adam. I had hoped that it had been his idea of a sick joke and that he would let it go.

I clicked on the notification in a panic.

Still thinking about that night? I am.

The second message was the video again. Us, stretched out on his bed. This time I didn't throw up. I wrote back:

What do you want?

I wanted to add 'Why do you hate me so much?' but I didn't want him to realise how powerless I felt.

An immediate response:

> I miss you babe. Don't you miss me?

No, Adam. I wish you were dead. I wish with all my heart that you had died with your phone locked and nobody could ever see this. Instead, I said:

> Why are you sending this to me?

He replied immediately:

> Hey don't freak out. It's just a reminder of what we had. I'm not after rent or anything.

Rent? What did that mean? I knew better than to ask him. I knew Adam. He was always after something. Right now I felt like he was using me but I wasn't sure how. Just for his own sick fantasy? That was the best thing to hope for. Please don't let him have shown anyone else. Please, please. The phone buzzed again. Please go away. Please go away.

But it was just Artie.

> See you at 7pm? What are you going to wear?

The poetry slam. Thank God. Something else to think about.

I tried to keep it in my head for the rest of the afternoon, crowding out the thoughts about Adam, and it almost worked. By the time the slam came around I was almost able to ignore them.

At Buster's our usual table was free and Artie stuck his coat over the spare chair and swiftly took a seat from another table to add to ours.

'Who're they for?' I asked. I had known Lucy was coming but that was only one extra chair.

'Lucy and Drew?' he said, as if I should have known already.

'Oh. Wow. I didn't realise Drew was coming.'

'Duh-uh,' he said, waving over my shoulder at Portia, who came over straight away.

'I'm glad yous kids are here,' she said. 'I've told Jewel to expect my best poets.'

Artie blushed and did his best Princess Di eyelash flutter. For God's sake! He was such an unashamed flirt.

'What can I get you? The usual?' said Portia.

'Yes, please,' we said in unison.

'So. Drew's into poetry?' I said as Portia walked away scribbling on her pad.

Artie rolled his eyes. 'Nooooo,' he said, 'Drew is into Lucy. Haven't you noticed the love affair of the century blossoming in front of your eyes?'

I ignored the sarcasm. Of course I'd heard about it. Lucy texted me as soon as it started.

'I heard that *she* asked *him* out,' said Artie, 'like, a couple of days ago?'

'Yep.'

'That's *huge*, Lottie. Have you ever known Lucy to ask anyone out?'

'No. She's never done that before.'

'She must *really* like him.'

He was right. Lucy wasn't the type to ask guys out. And she had sounded really excited about it when he'd said yes. I hadn't thought he'd be the type for a poetry night, though. Somehow, I didn't want to hear about it and I hoped that Artie wouldn't keep going on.

Portia brought our drinks just as the couple of 'the century' arrived. Lucy looked happy. I could make myself be happy for her. It couldn't have worked between me and Drew anyway. You don't go from Adam Bailey to a kid from Greenwood estate. Urgh. Why did I have to think about Adam again? And when did I become such a snob? I physically shook myself and took a sip of coffee, focusing on the caffeine buzz in my head.

'Hey,' said Drew, not quite meeting my eyes as he sat down.

I noticed it straight away, small as it was: the shiny red pin on his coat. He saw me looking at it and took his coat off.

'So. You're a Steward now?' I said.

It must have happened recently. There was an uncomfortable pause.

'Yeah. I suppose so,' he said.

'Oh, he's being modest!' said Lucy with a grin, squeezing his arm. 'Adam said he was a shoo-in. Exactly the type they want. I made him wear the pin tonight. I'm so proud of him.'

She giggled and Drew smiled but his face was flushed.

Good grief, Lucy, I thought. *How can those Neanderthals impress you so much?* But I knew how, because I had been impressed by them too. I had been on the periphery of their world, never quite allowed in, but identified as *elite* because of my connection to Adam. That was it, wasn't it? Lucy was me now. I hoped that Drew wasn't Adam.

'Great coffee,' I said, for something to say.

Artie scrunched up his face. 'It's the same as it usually is?'

Another pause, this time broken, mercifully, by an announcement from the front of the café. Applause broke out as Ms Jewel Nationality took to the small stage. She was easily 6 foot 5 in silver glitter spike-heeled boots that came up to her thighs. Artie's eyes were as big as plates. I couldn't help but grin. Jewel's tight green dress clung to her body, chest hoiked high and a waterfall of turquoise curls cascading beyond her shoulders. She smiled widely and spread her arms. 'Welcome all to the first Buster's Books and Coffee Poetry Slam!'

The applause was rapturous. When it had calmed down Jewel explained the rules. Out of the corner of my eye I saw that Drew and Lucy were holding hands. I tried to give Jewel my full attention.

'Over the next few weeks we're going to be bringing you the breast, I mean *best*, of Northern Ireland's poets!'

Laughter from the audience.

'Tonight we hold the first *heat* of the competition.' On 'heat' she held up both hands and wiggled her generous hips. 'There's still time to sign up! The rules are: No hate speech. And ... that's it. Sign up at the back. Don't be shy! If you've never done it before just remember, everyone's been a virgin once – even me!'

Everyone laughed again but the word 'virgin' made me cringe.

Artie elbowed me. 'What's up with you tonight?'

'Nothing!' I said, attempting a laugh which came out sounding fake as hell. 'Resting bitch face.'

He narrowed his eyebrows but turned back to Jewel Nationality as she finished explaining the rules of the competition. Each performer would have three minutes on the stage. After three minutes Portia would ring a bell and the poet would have to sit down. Judging would be done on two levels: applause and independent judging by a panel who sat at the side of the stage. Scores would be given out of ten. The bottom two acts would drop off. There would be several events. The winner would get a year's worth of free coffee at Buster's and a trophy, but, more importantly, the title of Buster's Books and Coffee Poetry Slam Champion.

Artie led the café in loud applause. He nudged me and I started to clap too.

'Cheer up, Lottie. By the way, I signed you up.'

I stopped clapping. 'You *what*?!'

It had been a little too loud. Jewel Nationality looked over at us. I beamed back and continued the applause. Out of the side of my mouth I growled at Artie. 'Why did you *do* that? You knew I didn't want to do this!'

He kept his eyes dead ahead, although the applause had stopped, and whispered back, 'So go and cross it off. There's time. But I think you should give it a go.'

He turned to face me, still whispering. 'You're good, Charlotte. Great, really. Come on, do it for me?'

Lucy leaned in to Drew, giggling. She clutched the lapel of his denim jacket, her red curls dancing with her laughter. He was laughing too. The red pin seemed to curve a smile at me in the candlelight. Fuck it. What did I have to lose?

I got up from the table.

Artie grabbed my arm. 'Hey, look. I'm sorry. Don't leave.'

Lucy and Drew looked up from their private joke.

'You're going?' said Lucy.

'No,' I told them, 'I'm going to the loo. I might be a minute or two – I'm going to have to look through my phone for a poem to read.'

Artie clapped his hands excitedly. 'Yasss!' He stood up to hug me. 'You won't regret this.'

'I'd better not.'

16. Drew

I definitely liked her. Lucy, I mean. She was nice-looking
and fun. A bit too chatty sometimes, but that was OK. I
had been thinking about asking her out when she asked
me. I said yes immediately. The only thing that had been
stopping me was this crush on Charlotte, who was clearly
not interested. And even if she had been, there was Adam,
who had basically told me not to go there. He was a bit of
a dick, but I didn't think much of it. One month into life
at Cooke's and I was still a fish out of water. The others
were mostly dead on but you did get the odd sneering look
at your crappy phone, the odd grunt of derision when you
took out your trainers for football. I didn't care about that,
though. I reminded myself that those people would last
about five minutes in our estate. They were afraid of me,
that was all.

Lucy had been friendly from the start. I never felt like
she was looking down on me. She was dead keen to come
down to the estate and meet my mates. No way was that
going to happen, though. Who knows what they might've
said? I mean, Dale would've been OK but some of them can
turn into immature idiots when there are girls around.

So how do you date a rich girl then? The estate was
out. And I couldn't take her anywhere expensive. She
had asked *me* out so I had to get in there first with a
suggestion, otherwise she might've gone for a posh restaurant or something.

Fancy a walk at Castle Park?

I texted as I lay on my bed.

Castle Park was the big park across town. The other side of Lisburn from Greenwood. It had a lake and it was far enough out that people didn't use it for drinking at night, so it was nicer – no broken glass, and they kept the flowers tidy. Best of all, it was free.

Sounds great! I'll get us some chips after.

I cringed a bit. She was trying to be nice, I knew, but she could obviously tell that I'd picked somewhere free on purpose. Oh well. I might as well get used to it. We arranged to meet the following morning, which was Saturday. A little shiver of excitement tingled down my neck. *This is what I need right now. Things are going really well.*

'You look nice!' said Mum the next morning in the kitchen. 'Steven, doesn't our Drew look the part today?'

I had only put on my good shirt. I didn't look any different to usual.

Dad raised an eyebrow. 'You going out to meet a girl?'

I could feel the heat creeping across my face. 'Give up, Dad! Gotta go.' And I legged it out of there with the two of them cooing and wolf-whistling behind me.

It was a really nice first date. It was sunny, and even though it was cold we got ice cream. We walked halfway round the lake, chatting about all sorts – our parents, our houses, our friends. She went on holidays and weekend breaks and she went to the theatre sometimes. She did so many things. It made me realise that if you're rich you always have something to talk about: places you've gone, experiences you've had. I went to the theatre one time with school – to see *Blood Brothers* at the Opera House. It was actually dead good but a bunch of kids in our class ruined it by being idiots and using the flip-up seats to launch popcorn into the seats behind us. They kicked us out at the interval, and we all got a week of detention because the teachers couldn't decide who was to blame. I always wanted to go back and see the rest of it. I thought about mentioning this to Lucy, but then thought I'd better not in case she suggested it. We both knew I couldn't afford stuff like that.

Halfway round the lake there was a bridge and we stopped to chuck bits of ice-cream cone into the water for the ducks. We leaned over the railing, both of us tossing in tiny pieces of cone. I wondered if, like me, she was trying to make the cone last because it was the perfect opportunity for a kiss. I thought back to my first kiss with Karen. We'd both been drinking, which made it easier. It was at Dale's house, completely unplanned. He'd gone to make toast and we were in his room playing video games. I went to pick up my drink and she'd used the opportunity to blow my character to bits.

'Oi!' I said, nudging her arm.

We'd both looked at one another, laughed and started kissing. When Dale came back he almost dropped his plate of toast. It had been a surprise to me too. We were girl-friend and boyfriend by the time we left his house.

This was different. It was a date. I didn't really know how to do a date. Were you meant to hold hands before you kissed? Were you meant to ask permission? Or would that sound creepy? I mean, *she* had asked *me* out so I could assume she wanted to kiss me, right? But maybe she didn't want to do it *right now*? Only a tiny pyramid of cone tip was left. I looked over to see how much she'd got just as she was throwing the end of it into the water. She caught my eye too, smiled and leaned in. I dropped the wafer onto the ground and kissed her. A pissed-off duck quacked loudly. She giggled. I knocked the wafer into the water with my foot, and we kissed again. It was nice. Casual. She tasted of vanilla.

'Come on,' she said, taking my hand and leading me off the bridge. 'I have to be at the shop by eleven.'

She volunteered in a charity shop on Saturdays. It was for her Duke of Edinburgh award. Something to put on the UCAS form.

'I'm going to a poetry thing with Charlotte and Artie next weekend. Want to come?' she said.

I really did. But the mention of Charlotte brought me back to that lunchtime with Adam and what he'd said about her. And there was something else too – something in the way he talked about people, boys especially, that made me think he wouldn't approve of a *poetry thing*. It wasn't like the way that my friends from Laney would take the piss if they found out I was taking a girl to a poetry event. It was something else.

'I'm not sure, Lucy. I might have football that night. Can I let you know?'

'Yeah. No worries.'

She didn't seem bothered. We kissed again, lightly, and walked off in different directions. Her to her charity shop, me to Greenwood.

A man's man. That's what Adam had said. He'd been talking about Butch, the football coach. It wasn't his real name, obviously, but that's what they called him. I didn't even know his real name.

'Butch is a man's man. Takes zero shit, you know? Great coach.'

He made it clear that a 'man's man' was something good, something you'd aspire to be. I thought of Don Antonio and the way he'd sigh sometimes when he finished reading a poem. The gentle way he'd nod when I got something right. His neat, crisp shirts. I guess he wouldn't make the grade as a *man's man* in Adam's books. It wouldn't have bothered me ordinarily. People like Adam didn't frighten me, and they don't impress me either. I like people who aren't bothered about stuff like that. Like Artie – the way he just looked so totally bored whenever a first-year made a comment about his hair or how he walked, like they were beneath dignifying with a response. I wished that I didn't need Adam's approval.

As I rounded the entrance to the estate I stopped to watch the kids playing football on the grass rectangle in the middle of the houses. Their hoodies were the goal posts. They looked serious, as if this was a big important match, not just what they did every Saturday. I thought about the kiss with Lucy. I wanted to go to that poetry night for so many reasons. It was pissing me off that there were some stupid invisible rules that meant I couldn't. I'd go, I decided. Adam didn't have to know. I didn't want him to end up controlling my life, but I could be careful, couldn't I?

I walked on past the match. One of the kids nodded to me as I passed. They knew I'd been good at football – a footie legend on the estate. It was a nod of respect.

17. Charlotte

I'll keep it under wraps
This tiger roaring to be set free
This girl you don't see
This mess that I call me
I'll make her look like a girl
Paint on two lips of pink
That smile and talk and
Glittered eyes that blink
And don't forget to act
As if you never think
But don't forget
To think ...
I'll hide my self
So you won't recognise
The person under this disguise
The truth lives in a body of lies
You see
It's not me
It's not me who cries
Not me who feels alone at night
Not me who doesn't know what's right
Not me who's giving up the fight ...

I might ...
I'll keep it under wraps
For now
I'll figure it all out
Somehow.

18. Drew

When she'd finished I could see that she was shaking. She looked up from the floor for the first time, and a smile broke across her face as the room burst into applause. She was good. Really good. Wow ... that poem. It was so raw. I took my hand away from Lucy's to join the clapping. Artie was jumping out of his seat yelling, 'Go, girl!' And Charlotte was blushing and smiling and then hugging Artie and sitting down again as the drag queen got on stage to introduce the next act.

'Charlotte,' I said, slightly breathless, 'that was amazing.'

'Thanks,' she said. 'I was so nervous.'

'You couldn't tell. You were great!' said Lucy.

It wasn't true. You *could* tell that she had been nervous. Her voice had been a bit shaky and she'd said it a bit too fast. But it didn't matter – the poem was brilliant. *She* was brilliant. Artie grabbed her hand as they settled and turned to watch the next act. The quick stab of envy as they turned away together was quickly dispelled when Lucy put her head on my shoulder. A tall thin boy, dressed entirely in black, his eyes obscured by his long fringe, was reading a doomy kind of thing about sea creatures. It was full of long words that sounded like they came out of a Charles Dickens novel. It must have been a metaphor for something but it was so obscure you couldn't tell what.

Lucy squeezed my hand.

'You enjoying it?' she said.

'Yeah!'

To be honest I was in awe of everyone on stage: Ms Jewel Nationality, even the skinny goth guy, and most of all Charlotte. All of them were just doing their thing. Openly being themselves, like it was something you could just *do*. After the sea-creatures poem was done it was another girl, Sylvia – this time with a fast-paced poem which she spat like every word was a dagger and she wanted to hurt you. It was a poem about being abused. She got louder and louder. We were transfixed. She was yelling at her abuser and we were in it with her. At the climax of the poem she suddenly stopped and started to whisper so quietly, and the room was silent and we heard every word. I looked around and some people were wiping their eyes. As she finished and the room started to cheer, Charlotte got up and headed off to the toilet. There was something in the way she got up – the speed of it, maybe, or the little jerk in her back as she stood to leave – something made me feel like she wasn't OK. But what was I going to do? Follow her? She came back a couple of minutes later. She smiled at us. I'd been wrong then – she was OK.

Lucy asked if I wanted another coffee. I felt guilty. Every time I was thinking about Charlotte, Lucy said or did something to remind me that I should have been thinking about her. It wasn't deliberate, obviously, but it felt like that. Luckily Lucy seemed to have no idea. In between poems she chatted about school, homework, who was seeing who. It seemed like she could always fill the gaps – there was no amount of time she couldn't speak into. I liked it. She kept the conversation going. On and on she chatted as the judges huddled, head to head, deciding the winners. There wasn't any time to worry about anything when Lucy was talking. But then she started talking about the Stewards, and I just didn't feel like going there. Not tonight.

'So have you had your first Steward meeting yet?'

'What? Em, no.'

'Oooh so you haven't been inducted.'

'What?' Shit, what was this? Were they going to make me do something weird to properly join? I'd heard about things like this, at American colleges, where they make people take their clothes off and stuff.

'Haha, don't look so worried!' Lucy tossed her red hair. It bounced around her shoulders like she was in a shampoo ad. I'd never met anyone with such shiny hair before. 'They won't do anything daft,' she went on. 'It's just to get to know you and explain things.'

'Explain things?'

'The "rules",' said Charlotte, doing air-quotes.

Had she rolled her eyes slightly too? I knew she thought Adam was a dick. Did she think I was a dick now too?

'Oh, right,' I said. 'I don't know much about it really.'

'Well, that's going to change *really* soon,' said Artie. 'You're one of the elite now, Drew. Wait till the first-years start bringing you caramel squares.'

I must have made a face because everyone giggled. Artie got up to get more coffee. I hadn't wanted to talk about it, but maybe I should try to learn some stuff before the *induction*.

'Lucy, Adam said something the other day and I didn't know what he meant. Something like he needed to talk to me about rent?'

Lucy frowned and hunched her shoulders. 'No idea. Do you know what that is, Charlotte?'

Charlotte's face was grey, her mouth slightly open. She paused, just very slightly, before saying, 'No idea.' I knew she was lying. Lucy hadn't noticed it, but I had. The word had freaked her out.

'I'm just going to help Artie with those drinks,' she said, getting up with the same little jolt she'd done earlier. Lucy turned back to me and shrugged. She hadn't noticed Charlotte's reaction. Or maybe I was reading too much into it. When she came back she seemed totally fine. She was smiling and Artie was grinning from ear to ear as he set the mugs down in front of us.

'Guess who's in the next round?' he said, settling back into his spot and pointing with both hands at Charlotte.

'What? That's great, Charlotte!' said Lucy, giving her arm a little squeeze. 'How do you know?'

'We overheard them talking,' said Charlotte. 'It's no big deal.'

But you could tell she was really pleased.

'It *is* a big deal! OMG! It's amazing!' Lucy was still clutching her arm.

Artie sipped his coffee. 'I told you it was good, didn't I?' he said to Charlotte.

I knew I should say something too. So I said, 'Congratulations.' I meant it. She deserved to go through.

'Really,' said Charlotte, 'I just got in by the skin of my teeth by the sounds of it. They were saying my delivery was crap.'

'They did *not* say that!' said Artie, rolling his eyes. 'What they said was that your delivery needed *work*, but that you *clearly* had talent.'

Charlotte blushed. *I bet she's used to acing everything*, I thought.

'Well, you're through, and that's the main thing,' said Lucy, ignoring Artie.

Charlotte smiled and said thanks. The judges were on stage shushing everyone, about to announce the list of people who'd made it. Charlotte's name was last, but when they called it our table yelled and cheered like she was a rock star. It was the first time since joining Cooke's that I had really felt part of something.

19. Charlotte

It should have felt amazing – to know that everyone who mattered was so pleased for me. But I couldn't shake the words out of my head: *Good, solid poem, but the delivery needs work*. That's what the judge had said. And the other two judges nodding along in agreement. Why did it bother me? I was through to the next round!

We hadn't even got up from our table to leave before I was thinking of Mum and how I could never actually *win* a poetry slam. It was just as well that I was sure to be put out at the next round. Imagine winning it and the local paper wanting to take my picture and me having to say no. And the prize. It was coffee for a year and a giant trophy. Where would I have hidden that?

The ten minutes between getting up to leave and actually reaching the door felt like for ever. I grinned and said thank you to everyone who congratulated me.

'Let's go and talk to Jewel!' said Artie, pulling me back from my escape.

'Nah, I think I'd better get home, Artie.'

'Come on!' he whined. 'It's early.'

Lucy and Drew stood aside to let Artie drag me back into the café. They said a quick goodbye and walked off, wrapped up in one another. *Lucky Lucy*, I thought. I didn't even mean because she was with Drew. Not really. It was just that Lucy seemed so light and happy; exactly the way I'd been when I started seeing Adam and thought he was my handsome prince. If only I'd known how boring it was going to be going out with him. Enduring his horrible mates and their constant jokes about drinking and shagging. Having to watch rugby matches at the weekend instead of films or box sets. At the beginning he'd brought me flowers and made my picture the screen saver on his phone. The romantic gestures tailed off after about a fortnight, and after that I felt more like his property, as if it was my job as Adam Bailey's Girlfriend to play along and do what was expected. Which obviously meant sex, on top of everything else. Stupid me for going along with it all. I hoped Lucy would have more wit, and I was jealous because I knew that she probably would. Drew seemed softer in a way than Adam. Less confident. Kinder.

'Jewel! Hi!'

Artie absolutely loved meeting new people. He is one of the only people I know who thrives on it. It makes him a great person to go out with.

'Oh, hello, you two!' At least a foot above us, Jewel beamed a wide smile encircled by a bright pink smear of lipstick. She put a hand on each of our shoulders and drew us in for a hug. 'Did you have a lovely night?' she asked, releasing us.

'Wonderful!' said Artie.

'Yes, it was really good,' I said, smiling as sincerely as possible.

'Ahhh.' She tipped her head to one side as if she was looking at a cute baby animal. 'Your poem was just brilliant.'

'Thank you.' I lowered my eyes and caught sight of her enormous spike-heeled boots.

Artie put his arm around my shoulders. 'Charlotte doesn't think her poem was that good.'

I glared at him.

'Really? Well, why not, hun? They wouldn't have put you through if it wasn't good.'

Both of them were looking at me now, their furrowed brows demanding an explanation. I could have killed Artie.

'I ... Well, I sort of overheard the judges talking and ... they said my performance wasn't good.'

Jewel smiled gently. 'They said it *needed work*, I believe.'

'That's what *I* told her!' said Artie. 'It wasn't *bad*, it just needs *work*!'

I glared at him again.

'You have to admit, you were a bit nervous!' he said, catching on to the danger he was in.

Jewel's forehead had gone wrinkly again. 'You really were very good, you know,' she said. 'Are you bothered by what they said?'

'No, not at all!' I said. But I knew that it was an obvious lie. I was never any good at lying.

'OK,' said Jewel. 'Gimme your number.'

'Em, OK ...'

'We can meet up. If you like,' she said, trying to enter my name and struggling slightly with her long red fingernails. 'Urgh, dammit. Look, you type it in.' She handed me her phone and continued talking. 'We can meet up here, for an hour maybe, and I'll give you some confidence tips. How does that sound?'

Artie's eyes lit up and he did a little bounce on his toes. I wished I could give her his number instead.

'Um, great. Thanks.' I handed the phone back to her.

'I won't be writing your poem for you. Just helping you get over those nerves, OK?'

'I'm ... so grateful, thank you.'

She smiled. 'You've got something. I'm just going to see if we can help you bring it out. Right?'

I nodded and smiled back.

We left soon after, and Artie was buzzing. As soon as we got round the corner he started jumping up and down and hugging me like I'd won an award. 'You realise what this means, right?' he said.

'Artie, no, what does this mean? It doesn't mean anything. She said she'd call me. It's nothing, I'm sure. She just wanted –'

'She just wanted to offer you some full-on drag-queen life coaching! How are you not excited about this? It's a dream come true!'

'It's *your* dream come true.'

'Wait.' He had stopped jumping up and down and his face was serious. 'You're joking, right?'

'Nope.' I started to walk on again, not wanting to look him in the eye. 'Artie, my mum would kill me if she knew I was in a poetry competition. How do you think she'd react if she found out a drag queen had offered to give me drama lessons?'

'It's not drama lessons!'

'Well, *full-on drag-queen life coaching* then.'

He rolled his eyes. 'She said she'd see you, once, to give you confidence tips. You could at least be grateful.'

'Grateful?' I stopped and looked straight at him. 'Artie, *you* made me go and talk to her. *I* wanted to leave. My mum –'

'*I* made you sign up in the first place. And you got through!'

I began to walk on.

'Look, I don't want to fight. Can we not?' Artie said in a gentler tone.

'Fine by me.'

We walked in silence to the train station. We were getting different trains, and Artie's was on the opposite platform to mine. Usually we'd sit opposite one another and text memes to make the other laugh as we waited. I didn't want to leave it like this and have to sit awkwardly pretending that he wasn't right across the tracks from me.

'I'm sorry,' I said before we went through the gates.

'Me too,' he said. 'I'm a dick.'

'You're not. And I *am* grateful. It's not your fault my mum's such a philistine.'

He smiled sympathetically and we hugged. 'Your poem was amazing, you know,' he said.

'Well, it must have been,' I said, 'because you haven't mentioned Mister Bubble Butt Perfect Pecs since I read it.'

Artie clutched his chest dramatically. 'The love of my life! If he's on this train it will be a sign. I will *die off.*'

I laughed. 'You're always dying off. See you on Monday.'

That's how we left it, and I went to my platform feeling light and glad until the phone pinged. It was one word. Actually, not even a word, just one letter. From Adam:

X

I swung round, as if he was somewhere close by, watching me. He wasn't, of course, but as the train roared into the station, blocking out the faint light from the moon, I couldn't shake the feeling. He was there anyway – in my head – and I couldn't get away.

20. Drew

That night stood out like a bright light as the winter crept in – going to school in the dark, coming home in the murky afternoon. But it wasn't just the lack of sunshine that was getting to me. I missed my friends. Dale had exams coming up. Every time I saw Karen she looked slightly more pregnant than the last. The pressure was piling on in school as well. I knew it would. The workload was expected.

Don Antonio was walking around the room handing back essays. I knew mine was bad. I'd done it about half an hour before leaving the house. The paper landed on my desk and I looked up at Don Antonio. His pursed lips said it all. I looked back at the paper. E. God. E. It was worse than I'd thought. I turned the paper over in case anyone else saw it. I caught sight of the bright red B on Charlotte's paper as she was turning hers over too. I wished mine had been a B. But it wasn't like her not to ace an essay. The room was unusually quiet. Don Antonio reached the end of the row and stood in front of the class, hands lightly on his hips.

'I don't know what's going on with you guys,' he said to us all, but eyeing Charlotte and me in particular. 'Let's call this an anomaly.'

He walked over to the portrait of Lorca that hung over his desk and pointed to him. 'He deserves better. Yes?' It would have sounded like a joke but the tone was serious.

'Repeat this for Friday and you *all* need to improve. That's all I'm going to say about it. Open at page forty-three.'

Nobody even groaned. We all just opened the book. I looked at Charlotte. She looked like she was about to cry. *It's only an essay*, I thought.

Eventually the bell rang and people began to scrape back their chairs.

'Not so fast!' said Don Antonio, handing out more papers.

Not more homework, surely?

'Spanish trip!' he said, reading our minds.

He was more cheerful now, making sure everyone had the letter. As people milled around, making their way to the door, reading the text, he chatted excitedly about it. 'It's a joint trip with the English department. We're going to Granada! Home of our poet!' He jabbed at Lorca again. 'We'll see plays. Read the letter!' he called as everyone piled out. 'Bring the forms back as soon as you can – first come, first served!'

Charlotte and I had let people go ahead of us – we were the last to leave. I stood aside to let her go first. She smiled.

'You going?' she said, waving the letter.

'Doubt it,' I said.

I didn't need to read the letter to know that there was no way we'd be able to afford it. But I didn't want her to feel sorry for me.

'I mean,' I continued, 'I don't know. I'll have to see if it clashes … with anything.'

She nodded. Too late. There was that sympathetic smile, reminding me that, no matter what, I wasn't one of them and I never would be.

'There might be a way you could go? I mean, maybe the school could subsidise it?' she said.

I didn't mean to physically wince, but honestly, it couldn't have been more humiliating if she'd done a public announcement in the cafeteria about how she'd never go out with anyone like me and how absurd it was that I should even think about her that way.

Get over it, Drew, I told myself. *You shouldn't be thinking about her in that way anyway.* I forced a smile, which I'm sure was grotesque, and told her not to worry about it, and then, Praise to Baby Jesus, we ran into Lucy. Linking arms with me and pecking me on the cheek, she said hi to Charlotte and we all walked off in the direction of the cafeteria. I was due to meet Adam there for my induction to the Stewards. Something I'd been dreading. But at least it was a different thing to think about.

'So!' said Lucy.

She always started everything as if she was about to tell you the most exciting news she'd ever heard. I wondered where she got her energy. I wondered why she liked me.

'Did you hear about this joint department trip to Granada? I'm definitely going. Are you?'

Charlotte's face went pale and I felt like I had to rescue her, even though it was me who was finding this whole thing excruciating. Everyone knew the truth anyway.

'I probably can't afford it,' I said. 'I'd love to, but …'

'Oh,' said Lucy, like she'd only just realised that the main consequence of having no money is that you can't afford things. 'I'm sorry, Drew, I just didn't think …'

'Look. Don't feel bad about it,' I said. 'It's just how things are. I'm lucky to be here. I know that, and –'

'Shut up!' Charlotte elbowed me playfully. '*We're* lucky that you're here, right, Lucy?'

Lucy nodded over-enthusiastically. 'Too right!' She squeezed my arm.

And then it was over and Lucy asked Charlotte about the next slam and Artie joined us in the cafeteria and I left them giggling away about something to do with Jewel Nationality and I went to find Adam for my induction.

'Good luck!' called Lucy, blowing me a kiss, and I waved at her as I walked away.

Adam was at the exit of the cafeteria. He had been standing with two of the other Stewards who followed us at a distance, like bouncers, as we left.

'How's it going?' he asked briskly. 'Noticed anything different, now that you're a Steward?'

'Em, not much,' I said.

'That'll change,' he said.

Finally we reached the place where the induction was to happen. It was a clubhouse at the very bottom of the playing fields. The old building, before the new sixth-form facilities were built.

'This is our place,' Adam said, pushing open the door. 'The Stewards' house.'

'You have your own clubhouse?'

'*We* have our own clubhouse.' He grinned as he led us in.

I couldn't believe it. It wasn't posh or anything, a few chairs and tables, a pool table, a nice-looking stereo and a hatch which led to a small kitchen. There were a couple of boys playing pool and they nodded to Adam as we came in. The 'bouncers' joined them at the pool table.

'Beer?' said Adam. He was talking to me.

'What?'

'Would you like a beer? There's a few in the fridge. Have one. It's your induction.'

He indicated a seat at one of the tables and went into the kitchen to retrieve the alcohol. The other Stewards chatted quietly with each other. They glanced up at me, serious but not unfriendly.

Sitting around having a beer in school uniform on school grounds? This was the weirdest thing I'd ever experienced. Adam came back and sat down in front of me with the beers. He could tell it was freaking me out a bit.

'Relax,' he said. 'It's cool.' He turned to the boys at the pool table. 'You all know Drew, right?'

The boys nodded towards me now. I knew one of them from my form class although I'd never talked to him. This all felt awkward as hell.

Adam offered me his bottle to clink mine against. Well, OK then. If he insisted.

Freezing cold fizzy lager. It was good.

'That's better.' He grinned. 'If you're worried about teachers catching us, don't. They gave us this place. We can use it for whatever our needs are as long as we don't bring the school into disrepute.'

'Right. But boozing is cool?'

'We're not boozing,' he said, stretching out his legs, his beer arm leaning on the table. 'We're just a group of gentlemen having an important meeting.'

I almost choked on my drink. 'I've never been called that before,' I said.

'Well, get used to it,' he said, totally deadpan. 'You're a Steward now. Anyway ...'

Adam downed his beer and straight away got up to get another. He held up the empty bottle and pointed at me with eyebrows raised. I held up my half-empty bottle and shook my head, *no thanks*. I still had one class left today, and after the E in Spanish I wanted to try to salvage something from the rest of the timetable.

'You probably want to know what this entails?' Adam said, returning to sit opposite me again. Now he was sitting up straight and I turned to face him. I guessed that the Important Meeting was about to begin. The pool balls clattered in the otherwise quiet room.

'OK, well,' he began, 'first of all, we're very glad to have you as a Steward. Your academic record is excellent ...' I cringed slightly, thinking of the paper in my bag. 'And you're doing well on the soccer team.'

I felt like he was my boss interviewing me about how my first month on the job had gone.

'It has also been noted,' Adam went on, 'that you've started a relationship with Lucy Campbell, and we're all very pleased to see this. Aren't we, lads?'

The boys looked up from their game and smiled.

I thought about his previous words about Lucy. *Great legs*. It made me feel slightly nauseous. But I let him go on. So far this was easy and I was grateful for the lack of nude challenges or weird tests of endurance.

'I'm just going to tell you a bit about the Stewards. Who we are, what we do and what you can expect. Then we're going to make an agreement. OK?'

'OK,' I said.

An agreement? I wasn't sure I liked the sound of that. But Adam was off, telling me the whole boring history of the Stewards, which he apparently knew because of his bigwig dad who was supposed to be the most class bastard to ever walk the earth or something. God. He went on about his dad so much I was tempted to ask him if he fancied his dad. And then I was off in a fantasy, to try and keep myself from yawning, about what would happen if I'd said that out loud to his face. I was just at the part where the ambulance was arriving to take me and my severed fingers to hospital when Adam said, 'And that's the story of the Stewards. Test next week.'

'Oh ... what?'

'Haha, just kidding!' he said. 'Your face!'

He took a swig of his beer. Adam was the type of person you couldn't second guess because it always felt like they were one step ahead. I didn't trust him.

'OK,' he continued. 'Down to the nitty-gritty.'

I leant forward. This I really did want to take on board, and I wanted Adam to know I was paying attention. This was my chance at the scholarship.

'The Stewards, as you know, are an elite group.'

I nodded.

'You've probably heard some rumours?'

'Not really,' I said. *Except that you're a pile of dicks, according to Charlotte*, I didn't add.

'OK, well. We represent Cooke's finest, academically and on the sports field.'

He really did sound like a dick. I had to admit it.

'We're expected to do well. Achieve well. Look well.' He looked at my tie and I straightened it. 'Behave well, or at least be *seen* to behave well, if you get my drift.' He smirked.

I nodded again. He meant *Do whatever you like but don't get caught or you're out*.

'Some rules. There aren't many, but they're serious. No second chances. You break a rule, you're out.'

'OK,' I said.

'First – confidentiality. This is key. What's said and done among Stewards stays among Stewards.' He nodded towards the boys who were racking up the balls, ready to start another game.

'No problem,' I said.

'I'm glad we understand one another,' he said, 'because what I'm about to tell you goes no further than our fellow Stewards.'

He was dangling his empty bottle of beer between his thumb and his forefinger, swinging it gently over the edge of the table as he looked me directly in the eyes. I felt like he was a mafia boss trying to suss out whether or not I was about to tout on him to the cops. I didn't feel afraid of him, though. Last year Dale's cousin touted on his drug dealer and he had both his knees broken outside their house in full view of the street. Real gangsters didn't have to hide in posh boys' clubhouses. Still, I was happy enough to play along. Whatever would make this lecture go faster and convince Adam that I was going to be a top Steward.

'Absolutely no problem at all,' I said.

'Good.' He got up to get another beer. 'You'll have one this time,' he called from the kitchen.

He wasn't asking, he was telling. I looked at the clock. Half an hour to the next class. He came out of the kitchen with four bottles. I knew as he sat down and cracked one open, sliding it over to me, that I was going to be late.

'As leader of the Stewards I've implemented a slightly new system to ensure maximum confidence in our ... confidences.'

I raised an eyebrow.

'You will know that we enjoy certain privileges as Stewards. You will be assigned a first-year student to bring your coffee at lunch break, and that student will also be happy to run errands for you. If you get a really smart one they might even be able to bring you a couple of these bad boys every so often.'

He smirked again, holding up the beer bottle. *Assigned?* There was no way I was going to have some mini-servant bringing me stuff. No fucking way.

'It takes a bit of getting used to, but believe me you'll enjoy it.'

I wanted to punch the smile off his face. But I reined it in and tried to smile back.

'I'm sure I will,' I said. 'You're right, though – I'm not used to stuff like that. Not at all.'

'Your teachers will go easy on the odd missed home-work. If you get a B+ you might find it converts rather easily to an A if you appeal. But they won't cover up for sloppiness. You still have to work. Particularly if you want that scholarship.'

I caught my breath and he noticed.

'I know that's why you're really here, Drew.'

Shit.

'Relax!' he said, slapping my arm. 'It's a good reason to be here. And as I said, you've proved yourself a deserving candidate so far.'

I was glad to hear it, but at the same time I knew it was going to take a lot for me to accept charity from someone who was so full of themselves. I tried thinking of Mum and Dad and how proud they were of me. I could do it for them. Who was I kidding? I wanted it for myself too.

'Thanks, Adam.'

'No problem. No problem.' He was tipsy now. 'So, yeah, there are perks to this game. And ... where was I?'

'New system.'

'Ah yes! Confidence!' He tapped his nose and winked. Definitely a bit drunk. 'Rent,' he said.

That word again. The one that had made Charlotte jump up so suddenly in Buster's.

'New rule. I'm collecting rent.' Adam put his beer bottle on the table and clasped his hands together. 'Each Steward is going to give me something.'

This is it, I thought. *This is the induction. The humiliation.* I braced myself.

'Like what?' I said. 'Money?'

He waved his hand in front of his face. 'No, no. I don't need that.' He looked mildly insulted.

'What, then?'

'Something much more ... binding.' He looked so pleased with himself. 'Jamesy gave me the passcode to his laptop.' He grinned. 'Ooof! You should see what's lurking in the depths of his hard drive! Barely legal, I can tell you.'

'What?'

He sat back again, his voice becoming louder. 'I know! I mean who can blame him, right? But he won't want it getting out. That's his rent.'

I looked at the boys by the pool table. They were smirking at one another. Well, Adam could have my computer password – there was nothing much on it in the way of porn. A couple of pics. Nothing weird. But he went on.

'Charles here made me a key for his own personal potting shed. Emphasis on the *pot*, if you see what I mean.'

One of the boys looked up from his game briefly and half-smiled. I wasn't sure how to read it. Did they really like Adam? Respect him? It was another world. Immediate expulsion if he was caught supplying drugs, surely.

What was Adam going to ask me for? I didn't really have any secrets. My poems? That was it. Hardly the scandal of the century. He wasn't ready to talk about my rent yet, though. On and on he went, telling me everyone's secrets, because now I was a Steward it didn't matter if I knew because I wasn't going to tell anyone, was I? Eventually he'd get something from me too – something to *ensure* that I wouldn't tell. He was absolutely loving the whole thing, laughing to himself as he spoke.

A text message flashed on my phone. I could see it was from Lucy. She was probably wondering how everything had gone. Fifteen minutes into class and I was still stuck here listening to this absolute *bellend*.

The tiny green light flashed urgently. Adam clipped the caps off another two bottles and it took me a second to register that he was holding one out to me.

'Am I keeping you from something important?' He passed me the bottle, nodding towards my phone.

'No, it's just Lucy. Probably wondering where I am, you know. Women!' I thought it sounded like something he'd say. I was right. He rolled his eyes.

'God, yes. How's it going anyway? Got any action yet?'

I almost spat out the beer. It wasn't that he'd asked. It wasn't as if the Greenwood lads wouldn't have asked. It was because it was *him*. As if I would've told him anything, given what he'd just told me about what he did with people's personal information.

He laughed. 'Come on, Andy. I won't say anything.'

Andy? Nobody called me that.

'No,' I said. 'Not yet.'

'Boo!' He gave me the thumbs-down sign. 'Get in there, lad! What about this trip, eh? Good opportunity to get some alone time with the missus, right?'

Until now I'd told Lucy I couldn't sleep with her because I was nervous our parents would hear and it didn't feel right doing it with our folks around. I knew I should have wanted to. I knew loads of guys would've given their right arms to sleep with someone like Lucy. But in all honesty I wanted to go on that trip because I'd never been abroad before. And because I wanted to go to the plays. And because Charlotte was going. I hated myself for it, but Lucy was the least of the reasons I wanted to go.

'I won't be going,' I said.

He nodded, a serious look on his face. For a second I thought that it was a nod of understanding, as if he had remembered that not everyone can just jet off to Spain without thinking about it. But then he said, 'Well, I can't blame you, mate. Poetry and theatres and all that. Sounds really boring. And having to hang around with that absolute *nonce* of a teacher as well. God ...'

He took a drink from his bottle.

I wanted to say something. I wanted to say everything that was bubbling up inside me. And I should have. I really should have. But I didn't. Instead I pretended to be like him. 'Yeah. Who'd want to go the whole way to Spain and have to spend all day going to plays and visiting museums? Just as well there's no way in hell I'd be able to afford it.'

I was not like him, though. I had let it slip.

Another pained face. This one looked genuine.

'Awwww, mate.' He shook his head and put the beer bottle down on the table. 'Mate, that is rough.'

'No, it's grand,' I said. 'I don't want to go. It'll be crap. If they were going to Ibiza for a week of clubbing then, yeah, I'd be up for that. But reading poetry and poncing around theatres? Nah. I'll give it a miss.'

But Adam wasn't listening. He was in another world. You could practically hear the cogs turning in his head. Suddenly he got up to his feet.

'Meeting over!' he announced. I looked at my phone: 3.15 p.m. School almost over too. Charles and the other boys set down their cues. I stood up. Adam stuck out his hand. A formal gesture, like this had been an executives' meeting in the boardroom and not a boozy chat in the clubhouse at the bottom of the playing fields.

I shook hands with him and he pulled me in and clapped me on the back. As his face moved towards mine his voice dropped to a whisper again. 'Don't you worry, Andrew. You'll be shagging your bird in Spain. The Stewards will make sure of it.' He broke away and grinned widely. 'Can't let the ladies down now, can we?' He winked.

'Thanks,' I said, cringing inside.

'That's what Stewards are for!' he bellowed, holding the door open for all of us so that he could lock up.

As we walked out of the clubhouse and towards the school my thoughts were confused and fast. Was I about to let Adam pay for my trip to Spain? Was that OK? He had the money, after all. Why not? Because he was awful, that's why not. Because I didn't want to owe him. Had I used Lucy to make this happen? Maybe it was the beer, or the freezing air that was turning to a hail shower, but I couldn't keep up with the words in my head, accusing me.

Adam turned to face me as we reached the school building. He spat on his hand and stuck it out again. Disgusting, but I knew what I had to do. This was our gentlemen's agreement. This was him saying 'I own you'. I returned the gesture and we shook on it.

'Stewards for life,' he said, and he sounded like he meant it.

21. Charlotte

I've never really loved school. I mean, who does? But I've never hated it either. Most of the time I felt pretty lucky to be at Cooke's. I got on well with the teachers and I'd never struggled with the work before. I wasn't *really* struggling now. I mean, it wasn't any more difficult than usual. It's just that now my brain space seemed really crowded. I had Adam in there constantly, replaying that video. When I tried to get away from him by talking to my friends I had loved-up Lucy going on about how Drew had 'sailed through' the Stewards induction and how he was sure to get the scholarship, or Artie asking me if Jewel had called. I said no, but actually she had. Well, she texted, so it wasn't a complete lie ... We had arranged to meet up at Buster's after school. Despite myself I was looking forward to it. I had told Mum that I had to do extra English.

This was also not a complete lie. Miss Robinson had given me a bunch of reading to do after my last homework.

'I'm concerned about this,' she said with a sad smile, holding up my essay on Heaney. She had asked me to stay behind after class. First time ever.

'I almost got an A,' I said.

The hint of a smile disappeared. I hadn't meant to be rude.

'Sorry,' I said.

'B+ is good, of course,' she said in a gentle tone, 'but you and I both know that you are an A* student.'

I had no answer.

There was a pause.

'Is everything OK with you?'

The sympathy in her voice was too much. I could feel myself starting to wobble. *Breathe, Charlotte. Don't cry, for goodness sake.*

'Yes,' I managed to say. 'Work is a bit ... I mean, this term has been hard work.'

She nodded. 'A level is hard work. You're doing well. Look, I don't want one of my top students getting stressed, OK?'

I nodded, unable to look her in the face. She was being so nice. I was trying really hard not to cry.

'If you find things are getting on top of you I want to know, OK?'

I nodded again. My shoulders were starting to shake. A tear tipped at the corner of my eye and I wiped it away quickly. She noticed, of course.

'None of this stuff is worth getting down about, Charlotte.' A gentle smile. 'I'll let you go to lunch. Here's an essay to read ...' She handed me a folder. 'And take this ...' She hunted in her drawer for a minute and pulled out a copy of *District and Circle*. 'Read this one ... and write down your thoughts about it.'

She handed me the open book. The poem was called 'Anything Can Happen'.

'It might seem like a sad poem but think about the wider implications of it, Charlotte – *anything can happen* ... even if things seem impossible right now.'

I nodded and glanced at the poem. Something about tall towers falling.

The lump in my throat blocked any words.

Her brow wrinkled. 'You make sure and come to me if you're not OK, will you?'

I nodded again. I knew how to do this. I knew how to work. You get your head down, you block out everything else, you immerse yourself in the text. I wondered if she knew what to do when the method of shielding yourself from stress that you've used your entire life suddenly breaks? When you're looking at a poem and the words all seem to be speaking about the thing you're trying not to think about? I couldn't ask her that, could I?

I managed to get through the rest of the day. Even though I needed my file for Spanish I didn't go to my locker at the end of school in case I bumped into Artie, or anyone. I headed for Buster's the long way round.

There wasn't anyone in the café apart from a man sitting on his own sipping from a large mug. I looked around for Portia. I could hear her clattering around in the tiny kitchen. I stood at the counter for a minute waiting for her, rather than trying to shout over the noise of pans clattering.

'Charlotte?' The voice came from the corner. I recognised it and turned around. 'Over here, love.' The man was beckoning me from behind his giant mug. 'It's me, Jewel.'

'Oh, I totally didn't recognise you,' I said, relieved that 'Jewel' was here, but slightly spooked by her voice coming from this other person's body.

He was younger than I thought he'd be for a start. Legs crossed. Chinos and a plain blue shirt with a mauve cardigan. He looked more like a librarian than a drag queen. But he smiled and I relaxed and sat down.

'Jason,' he said. 'You can call me Jay. Either's fine.'

I smiled.

'Portia's making soup.' He rolled his eyes playfully. 'I'll get you a wee coffee when she comes back.'

'Thanks,' I said.

'You're nervous about all this, aren't you?'

I nodded.

'But you want to perform?'

'Yes.'

I did. I really did. Being up there, saying my own words, nobody relying on me, no team to let down. And I could say whatever I wanted to say. Anything at all. I loved it. But there was a problem.

'It's just ...' I started. I might as well tell him. 'Well, my mum ... she's against this kind of thing.' He raised an eyebrow. 'Poetry, I mean.'

I didn't want him to think Mum was a homophobe or something. I mean, she definitely wouldn't have approved of me hanging out with a drag queen in my spare time, but that was more to do with snobbery than anything else. Mum approved of *everyone*, as long as they were academically minded and heading for one of the professional careers she deemed suitable for her only child. Drag artists were not on the list.

'Go on,' said Jay. 'This stuff is important.'

He was sitting right back on his chair, his face serious but soft, somehow. He was only paying attention to me. He didn't know me, but he was interested. He was listening. God, I wanted to say it all then – to tell him about school and Drew and most of all about Adam. And I almost did. I almost said it to this total stranger. But instead Portia came out of the kitchen and, although Jay was still listening, I broke the moment by getting up. 'I'll just get that coffee. Right back.'

In the time it took to order and return to my seat I had shaken myself out of the desire to purge. I could tell him some things but not everything. What advice could he have given about Adam anyway? Tell the principal? My mum? The police? As soon as Adam was confronted about it I knew he'd have circulated that video in seconds.

So I sat down again, and Portia brought my drink over, and I told Jay about the pressures of school and about Mum and how she needed me to be this big academic success, which left no room for anything else, and how she'd be so angry if she even knew I was here.

'I wish I could just wear a disguise, like you. Then I could be whoever I wanted,' I said at last.

Jay's mouth turned up slightly at the edges. 'Drag isn't quite like that,' he said. 'For me it's less of a disguise, and more like a way to explore part of me that just doesn't quite work with these chinos.'

'Like, your feminine side?' I was interested now. And glad that we weren't talking about me for a minute.

'More like ... I don't know. There are things I can say and do as Jewel that just wouldn't have the same impact if I was performing them as myself, even though I might want to say the exact same things. She helps me to be myself in some way. So I'm not hiding when I'm Jewel. In some ways I'm more Jason than I am right now.'

He leaned in then. The café was still empty but he whispered as if he was telling me a big secret. 'Some people never learn how to do that, you know. They go their whole lives wearing a disguise that looks just like them. And they fool *everyone*, even themselves. It's sad really.'

'I know what you mean.'

'Charlotte, listen.' He was still leaning close. 'Whatever is inside you of yourself, the good stuff, whatever it is that nobody else can see – that belongs to you. Nobody can steal it. That's the secret to being bold on stage. You can't destroy what's really important about you. So you're free – you can do whatever you want.'

We sat in silence for what seemed like minutes. It was so quiet that I could hear Portia softly humming 'You Are My Sunshine' in the kitchen. I wanted to sit like this for longer. What if I could do that? What if everything could be that simple? Just to admit that I wasn't this person that everyone thought I was. To disappoint my mum. To tell Adam no. To let go. To fail. To be free.

'Are you OK?' Jay said.

I put my hand to my face and realised I'd been crying.

'No,' I said. 'I wish I could be like that. Like you, I mean. But I don't think I can.'

He looked sympathetic. Or sad. It was hard to tell which.

'You don't have to be like me,' he said. 'You have to be like you.'

I nodded. He didn't understand. I couldn't.

'Maybe,' he said, after we sat in silence for some time, 'maybe you can start by just being a *little* bit braver. Not changing everything. Just stepping out a *little* bit. How does that sound?'

It sounded impossible. But I nodded my head and smiled at him. I felt so heavy. I could have fallen asleep right there, at the table.

'I have to go now,' I said, wiping my face again and standing up.

Jay looked a little surprised.

'I know we haven't been here for long,' I said, 'but it was very helpful. Thank you.'

He stood up too. 'Give us a hug then.'

He hugged me and I could smell the remnants of Jewel's perfume on his shirt.

'You're in the next round!' he said, releasing me from the embrace. 'Try to enjoy it, OK?'

'Thanks, Jay. I'll see you then.'

And even though I wasn't sure that I would, I knew that at least I wouldn't stop writing, because I wanted to try it out, at least privately, writing something bolder, *being* someone bolder. I wanted to try.

22. Drew

Nothing was said about my absence from class. Lucy said that Adam would have 'sorted it'. Obviously I wasn't going to start complaining about that, but it made me uneasy. I could handle myself. I didn't need some posh boys' club to help me out. But what I really hated was how everyone else started treating me. I went from being pretty much invisible to having kids I didn't know saying hi to me in the corridors, even holding the door open. I hated it. Hated thinking that somehow I'd risen to a higher-status position for no reason at all. At home in our estate the lads would never understand this. Cooke's was so different. It was like the students here just automatically respected authority. Or maybe it wasn't respect. I thought back to what Adam had said about the 'rent'. Maybe it was fear.

I was outside the sixth-form centre on one of the park benches at break time, sitting in the sun, wishing I had a cold beer, when this tiny boy walked up to me. 'Are you Drew?'

His uniform was so smart and clean, his haircut so neat. He looked like one of those Lego figures.

'Yeah,' I said. 'Who wants to know?'

'I brought you this,' he said.

He reached in his bag and pulled out a can of Coke and handed it to me. It was ice cold.

'Em. Nice one,' I said.

I sat up and opened the can, holding it out to offer him a drink. He looked shocked and shook his head.

'So, what's this all about?' I said.

But I knew before he answered. This was my *assigned first-year*. I gulped down the sweet fizz. One can of Coke I could deal with, but I didn't want this kid following me around, bringing me stuff.

'I'm Christopher,' he said. 'I'm to bring you things. At break or lunch. Do you want anything later?'

'No!' I said, probably a bit too aggressively.

His eyes widened.

'I mean ... Look, Christopher. I'm not really into this whole servant thing. I don't really want you bringing me stuff. Thanks for the Coke, but ...'

'But I've got to!' he said, and he had this look that I couldn't figure out.

I could see his eyes starting to fill up. He had a metal badge the same as mine, only the 'S' was smaller and it was purple instead of red.

'You don't have to –' I said.

'I want to.'

He wiped at his eye. For God's sake. What was I meant to do?

'OK,' I said.

He grinned. 'Good,' he said. 'Then, what do you want for later?'

I shrugged. 'Another Coke?'

'Great!' he said. 'I'll bring it to you here then? At lunch?'

'OK.'

He straightened out the bottom of the blazer and for a minute I thought he was going to bow or something but he spun off across the playground. The sun went behind a cloud and I headed back inside. Who was paying for all this Coke and stuff? The Stewards? Christopher? He could probably afford it, but it still wasn't right.

Inside the common room Adam caught my eye and raised his coffee cup. I nodded and looked around for anyone else to sit with. Charlotte was at the back talking to Artie. Her laugh seemed warm and inviting, like you wanted to know the joke so you could join in. *It is not OK to be thinking like this.* I was just about to head to the library when Charlotte saw me and called me over. I looked back to Adam. Surely he wouldn't mind when Artie was with us? That made it safe, right? I could just make sure that I was paying Artie some attention too.

I didn't have to worry. Artie was in full flow, going on about some 'ho' that was after his man (the guy from the bus). Said 'ho' was a boy from our school who Artie reckoned was way beneath the bus guy.

'I swear, Charlotte, if my man gets with that little squirt I am going to have to cancel the Gay Community on grounds of a taste crisis.'

Charlotte was cracking up. 'Just ask him out, for the love of God!' She giggled. 'None of us can stick this any more, can we, Drew?'

'Um, I don't know. No?'

'Drew!' She whacked me with one of the cushions. 'You're meant to be on my side! Artie needs an intervention!'

I smiled. It was the happiest I'd seen her since the poetry night. Ever since then she'd seemed really quiet. I'd assumed it was about work. Everyone's workload was hiking up. We were going to have a test on Lorca and the Spanish Civil War next week. But now she was relaxed. More like she was when I'd first met her.

'Sorry.' I shrugged. 'Yes, Artie, you should ask this dude out. Do you know his name yet?'

Artie gasped dramatically and Charlotte dissolved into fits of giggles again.

'Of course I know his name!' he said. 'It's Crispin. Isn't that gorgeous? Who else is called Crispin! And – I got his number.'

It was Charlotte's turn to gasp. 'Whaaat? You didn't tell me that! How did you get it? Phone him! Phone him *right now*, Artie! *Carpe diem!*'

Artie pulled a face.

'Anything can happen!' said Charlotte. 'Just do it!'

'I will, I will ...' he said. 'And if you must know, I asked him for his number.'

Charlotte did a mock faint which made us all laugh. 'You *asked him for it*?'

Artie smiled, open-mouthed, and did a 'ta-daa!' signal with his hands.

'OMG, Artie!' said Charlotte. 'You not only spoke to him, after all this time, but you asked him for his number and he gave it to you and why-the-hell-haven't-you-called-him-already?'

'Should I?' said Artie. 'I'm scared ...'

'YES,' Charlotte and I both shouted in unison.

I glanced around. Everyone was looking over at us, including Adam. When I caught his eye he frowned slightly.

'I'd better go,' I said, getting up. 'Lorca's calling me from the library.'

They waved me off.

'You'll be at the poetry slam later, right?' said Artie. 'It's the big one – winners get to the final!'

'Oh, shut up, Artie, like I'm not nervous enough already!' said Charlotte, hiding behind a cushion.

'I'll be there,' I said. 'You'll be brilliant, Charlotte.'

On the way to the library my phone pinged. A text, from Dale.

> Karen n Jonny's engagement do at the
> weekend. You up?

Was I up for this? I didn't know. Part of me wanted to. A party right now? Yes, please. Lucy wouldn't be there. It could just be me and my old friends having the craic, getting drunk, doing stupid stuff. But *Karen n Jonny*. I hadn't thought about Karen for a while now, but here she was again, dropping in to remind me how far away from my old life I was. *Karen n Jonny. And baby.* Maybe I should just steer clear. It was only going to be round someone's house anyway probably. I could see my old friends some other time, couldn't I? It didn't have to be this night, with Karen there. I texted back:

> Dunno. Might give it a miss.
> I have a load of homework.

Dale texted back:

> Homework? Come on. It'll be a banger.
> Karen's ma hired the community centre.
> They're getting a band and a load of booze.
> You're going. OK?

I had to smile. Dale wanted me there and that was good enough. I texted him back:

> OK. Saturday? What time?

It was such a casual decision. Something to look forward to. A bit of craic with the lads. If I'd known how that party would turn out I wouldn't have gone in a million years.

23. Charlotte

How honest do you want me
To be?
Do you want to know
What I really think?
What I think is that
I think
You *don't*.
What I think is that
I think
You won't
Like it
If I tell it.
You won't hear it
If I speak it.
You won't see it
If I show it.
You won't recognise me
Cos the lies that disguise me
Are the colours of your whole world
The colours of every girl I know.
Do you want to know
Me?

Think about it, carefully,
You might lose yourself
When you see
What you see,
When I take off 'me',
You might figure out
That what I've rejected
Is what's reflected
When I look at you.
So think about it,
Slowly now,
I can tell you all what's true.
But if I do,
It might
Destroy
You.

24. Drew

We clapped like mad. We stood up and cheered. She was amazing. I mean, the poem was amazing. But she was too. It was like you couldn't separate the things she was saying from *her*, standing there on the stage. It was different to how it had been. She was more *alive* or something.

'Doesn't she seem more *alive* this time?' I said to Lucy.

Lucy made a face as she stirred her latte with a long spoon. 'What?'

'Nothing,' I said. 'Charlotte was great, though, wasn't she?'

'Amazing!' said Lucy, smiling.

Lovely Lucy. Genuinely happy for her best friend. She never had bad thoughts about anyone. Or if she did she never shared them. Every time we went out she said nice things about her friends. Kind things. It was so different to anyone I'd ever gone out with before. She seemed so innocent in some ways, like she'd never really had her heart broken or been bullied. It made me feel warm towards her, but it also felt like a huge responsibility.

'When are we going to do it?' she had asked the last time we were together.

'We can't do it here,' I'd said, sitting up straight on the bed where we'd been kissing. 'Your folks are downstairs.'

'We could be quiet. Don't you want to?'

'I do!' I lied. 'I just don't want to do it *here*.'

She'd rolled her eyes then, but it was in good humour, as if I'd told some rubbish joke or I was adorable-but-annoying. I hated myself for how nice she was. And I could have done it, of course I could. But it wasn't right, because I wanted Charlotte.

And now here was Charlotte, walking back to our table at Buster's after her incredible performance. She'd been speaking to one of the judges.

'I'm through!' she whispered, unable to stop herself from doing a little dance as Artie jumped up to hug her.

'Well,' said Artie, 'I for one am not surprised, because *that* was stunning.'

Lucy and I nodded and joined in the appreciation. Charlotte's eyes were glittering with excitement. The candlelight was making her red dress glow but I half wondered if she would've lit up the place in pitch dark. I wanted to hug her too. Instead I took Lucy's hand.

'Well, look,' she said, sitting down, 'I did get through. But I'm bottom of the ones who did.'

'What? How is that even possible?' Lucy said, looking genuinely upset.

'There's still something missing,' said Charlotte. Her face tensed up and she dropped eye contact with Lucy.

'They said that?' said Artie. 'That there was something missing?'

'No,' said Charlotte, brightening and looking up again. '*I* know there's something missing.'

'There's not!' the three of us said together.

Charlotte laughed. 'You lot are the best,' she said.

She had brushed it off and nobody else had really noticed, but there had been a moment, just a second or two, where she wasn't OK. *She puts herself under so much pressure*, I thought. *Always wanting to be perfect. I know I'd never be good enough for her. Even if it was possible ...*

'Earth to Drew!' Lucy was tapping my head lightly with the latte spoon. 'What's your order, space boy?'

I was glad nobody could see me blushing in the darkness of the café. I would need to be careful. I could save my thoughts about Charlotte for my poems. No need to indulge myself when I was with Lucy. The last thing I wanted to do was to hurt anyone.

25. Charlotte

Things felt like they'd lifted a bit the day after the slam. We were on late lunch, sitting in the sixth-form centre, and Artie was making me laugh so hard. He had called his man to arrange a date.

'Well hallelujah!' I said.

'All right, all right.'

'Oh my God, Artie. Are you ... are you actually *shy*?!'

'Shut up!' he screamed, throwing his hands to his face. 'I'm going to the toilets! Stop it!'

Uber-confident Artie, suddenly coy and embarrassed. I wish I'd taken a picture.

Thirty minutes. That's all I got. For that thirty minutes I was completely free. The excitement of the poetry slam was a warm feeling in my chest and it made me find Artie even funnier than usual. I had almost completely forgotten about everything else.

Clearly it was too much for Adam to see me happy because as the bell rang and I got up to leave he blocked my path.

'Excuse me,' I said, avoiding his glare.

'Let's talk,' he said, not moving.

I glanced around. Nobody had noticed. Hardly anyone was left. Just the geek group who were crowded round a tiny speaker listening to something you could hardly hear. The second bell went and they left through the other door.

'I have English now, sorry, I can't.'

He didn't move.

I looked up at him. 'Adam, can you move, please?'

'This will only take a minute. Sit down.'

I was scared then. Seeing him face to face like this. I couldn't do anything else. I sat. He sat beside me. *Too close*, I thought.

'What do you want, Adam?' I tried to keep my voice steady.

He put his hand on my knee. 'You. Of course.'

No. No. No. If you can scream silently then that is what I was doing. I wanted it to explode out of me, to force him away. But I couldn't. I tried to move my leg but he held it steady with his hand.

'This isn't right,' I whispered.

'It is, Charlotte. We should never have broken up. We are meant to be together. I sent you the video. To remind you.'

Something snapped inside me then. I stood up quickly. 'No. You sent me that video to frighten me. And you're frightening me now. You have to stop this.'

I went to walk off and he got up and grabbed my arm, spinning me around towards him. He was so strong. I tried to break away but it hurt.

'You're wrong, Charlotte. I don't want to scare you.' I wanted to tell him to stop saying my name. 'Actually, I love you, and if you thought about it you'd realise that. If I didn't love you I'd have shown that video to everyone by now, wouldn't I?'

'Let me go. Please.'

My voice was barely audible. *How do women scream when this happens to them?* But that's what you're meant to do – scream, shout, use your fingernails. All I could do was whisper 'please'.

'Just give me a hug. That's all I want. Just a hug.'

If I did it I could get away. I could tell someone. Just a hug. 'OK.'

He pulled me in to his chest. Tight. He smelt of the rugby changing rooms – expensive deodorant, sweat. He sighed. I tried to breathe. He tightened his embrace, hands pressing my back, locking my chest into his, my stomach to his own. I felt his belt against me. His breath on my neck.

'This is nice, isn't it?' he whispered.

I didn't answer.

He let me go.

I crumpled into the seat.

'Thank you,' he said. 'I'll text.'

I nodded without looking at him, tears falling into my lap. He left and I sat there, alone.

26. Drew

> What is a good person?
> Is it someone who tells the truth?
> Or someone who lies,
> So that good people don't get hurt?

I was trying to write a poem. I kept scrunching up the paper and starting again. I didn't know how to say it, even in Spanish. I didn't know how to think it. The phone lit up. I knew it was going to be either Lucy or Adam. It was Adam. He'd been texting me on and off since the induction.

Adam: Alright lad? Party at Jamesy's tomorrow night. You can bring Lucy if you like. Plenty of rooms for top shaggers!

Luckily, I had a good excuse.

Me: Ah, sorry I can't. Friend's engagement party.

Adam: Engagement? Jesus. What age are they?

Me: 17

Adam: God. So many birds – why would anyone get married at our age?

Me: They're having a baby.

Adam: Bloody hell. That's his sex life ruined then.

I didn't want to think about Jonny and Karen's sex life but at least it was better than Adam grilling me about my own, or the lack of it. His texts were always about getting off with 'birds' or getting drunk with the rugby lads or playing rugby ... I started to wonder why so many girls wanted to sleep with him. It definitely wasn't for the exciting conversation.

Me: Yeah I suppose so. I'd better go – Spanish coursework. You know how it is.

Adam: Don Wang? Yeah I know. He likes to think he's above the Stewards but he'll get what's coming in the end. You know he tried to get me suspended one time for telling a joke about him being a pedo? Total snowflake.

He really seemed to hate Don Antonio. He was always making homophobic remarks about him. It made me uncomfortable, but I never contradicted him. I went back to writing the poem.

27. Charlotte

Mum wasn't home, thank God. I made myself a coffee and let it go cold. Normal people had coffee. I did not feel normal. I opened Mum's drinks cabinet and poured myself an inch of rum, then another inch, and topped it up with Coke. It was sweet and I sat down and sipped it and felt myself finally breathing out.

Artie had found me, sitting in the same spot where Adam had left me, after school. I hadn't been able to move for an hour since Adam went to class. I'd stopped crying, but Artie told me later that I was just sitting there, staring into space. He thought I might be having a seizure or something. He'd managed to get me to talk to him and all I could say was 'Don't leave me alone?' and he'd sat there for another half hour until I'd let him take me home with a promise to text him when I was feeling better.

I was trying to feel better. I left down the drink and grabbed my journal and a pen.

Here are the important things, I wrote.

> I am still alive
> He did not rape me
> Nobody has seen the video

What else? *Come on. Pull yourself out of this, Charlotte.*

> I am smart and hardworking
> I haven't done anything wrong
> I have good friends

Could I tell them? For a second I thought of Lucy and wondered if she'd believe it. She was so impressed by Adam and his followers. And now her boyfriend was one of those followers. And it wouldn't be fair on Drew – he wasn't really one of them, was he? He just wanted to go to university. He wasn't so different to me – both of us needed Adam in some way. I wondered if that thought made him feel like vomiting too.

I heard the door opening. Mum was home early. Imagine what she'd think if that video got out. She'd be crushed. She was always telling me to be careful. To choose boys well. Not to give them everything they wanted. She had no idea I'd slept with Adam. That alone would have disappointed her, even though she, like everyone else, thought we had been a great match. She'd be delighted if she thought we were getting back together. I wanted to scream. I felt insane. I needed to tell someone. I had to.

'That you, Lottie?' called Mum from downstairs.

Try to sound normal, Charlotte.

'Yeah,' I called back. 'Just doing homework.'

'Good girl!'

I lay on my bed and scrolled through my messages. One from Artie.

> You OK?

Poor Artie. It must have been awful finding me like that and not knowing what had happened. What if I told him? No. There's no way he could keep it to himself. And then the video would be out there. I couldn't. I texted back.

> Just hormones! Sorry for scaring you.
> I'm good, I swear.

I wondered what it would be like to be able to plan an attack on Adam. To really hurt him. To see him suffer.

Artie: If you're sure …

Me: I am. Love you lots like jelly tots. Xxx

Artie: Love you too biatch. Xxx

I let the fantasy fill my head. Kicking Adam. Punching him. Hearing him beg me to stop. What would it be like to feel strong? I hated him, but I envied him too. If I had his power nobody could ever touch me.

My phone buzzed again. It was Jay.

Great performance the other night. Still work to do though. You on for a confidence session next weekend?

Me: Yes. And I want you to turn me into a man.

28. Drew

If the party had ended after the first three hours it would have been perfect. We'd all have left, half-cut, laughing too loudly, slagging each other within an inch of our limits. We drank too much cider, smoked too many cigs, told stupid jokes that didn't even make sense. The band were great. They played a bunch of songs everyone knew in between their own. Dale thought they were crap.

'Look at him there,' he said, nodding towards the lead singer. 'He thinks he's class.'

'He *is* pretty good, like,' I said.

'Yeah but he thinks he's better than us, doesn't he?'

I knew what Dale meant. The singer was giving it stacks but he was hardly looking at the audience. Still, who cared? They were here to bring the party. Dale always got too worked up about what people from outside our estate thought of him.

The community-centre hall looked good as well. Karen's mum had got a ton of orange and yellow crepe paper and made giant flowers which they'd stuck all over the walls. At first it looked like someone had let a bunch of primary kids decorate their classroom. But when the band started and the coloured lights came on it looked brilliant – like a different world.

I spotted Karen straight away She was definitely pregnant-looking now, which was weird. I mean, everyone's seen a pregnant woman before, that's nothing unusual, but it wasn't just any woman, it was Karen: Karen who had been *my* Karen not that long ago, and now she had an actual baby inside her. Suddenly the alien landscape on the walls seemed to make perfect sense.

'Seen enough?' It was sarcastic but she was smiling.

'Oh, um, sorry. I didn't mean to stare. Hi!' I handed Karen the present I'd brought and kissed her awkwardly on the cheek.

'Thank you!'

She unwrapped it. I had no idea what you get your pregnant ex-girlfriend who's about to get married. The lads had all brought bottles of vodka. Great for Jonny, but not much use if you're the pregnant one. Still it seemed like a less weird present than mine, which was a black iron photoframe with Celtic knots and green stones embedded in the twists of metal. It was a grown-up present. Too grown up for us, really. I knew as soon as I'd given it to her that it was weird. But actually she seemed really touched.

'It's us,' she whispered, looking at the picture in the frame.

It wasn't just us, of course. I didn't give my ex a framed picture of the two of us for her engagement party. I wasn't a complete prat. It was a picture of the whole gang a while back when we were all still at school together. It was the eleventh night – the night when all across Northern Ireland people light the massive bonfires they've been building before the Twelfth of July parades the next day. My mum had taken the picture with her phone, so it wasn't the sharpest photo ever. But it was a good one. Me, Karen, Jonny, Dale, Kyle, Al, Lisa. Everyone with a bottle or can. Everyone laughing. We were on our way to the bonfire. It had been a brilliant night, messing about, talking crap. That was the night that I told Karen I loved her. I'd never said that before to anyone – not even my mum and dad – but I meant it. She looked great that night – white T-shirt and skinny jeans, her hair left down when she normally wore it up, pale-pink lipstick when she never usually wore make-up at all. When the bonfire went up and everyone cheered I saw her watching the little kids at the front to make sure they didn't do anything stupid. I had pulled her in and kissed her and said *I love you*. She said it too. By the following year Karen and I had split, and Lisa and Al too, and we all still went to the bonfire but it wasn't as good.

'You like it?' I said.

'Yeah.' She stopped staring at it and looked up at me.

I couldn't be sure, but it looked like she was on the verge of tears.

'I love it. Thanks.'

'OK, well,' I said. 'Have a good night, then.'

And I wandered off to find the lads, wondering if we'd had what Artie might call a 'moment'.

I shook it off, though. The last thing I needed was some weird memory of a thing that was definitely in the past ruining a good night and making my life way more complicated than it was already. That's why I should have left that party when I knew I'd had a bit too much to drink. And that's why, when Dale nudged me to alert me to the sight of Karen and Jonny having a row in the corner of the dance floor, I should have ignored it and told myself that it wasn't my problem. And when Karen threw her drink over Jonny and stormed out of the room, I should have headed the other direction. To the bar. Or maybe even home. Definitely home. I shouldn't have gone after her. And when

Dale was shouting, 'Drew, leave it. It's not your problem, mate,' I should've listened.

But I didn't. I followed her.

I walked right past Jonny. He looked really wrecked, possibly high, completely wired. And me, my head was spinning too. I knew I was drunk, but not so drunk that I didn't know that this was crossing a line. I could see the fire escape open at the end of the corridor and I had that whole corridor to tell myself to go home. But then I was at the end of the corridor and it was so dark and the moon was cut like a scythe, gleaming over the carpark, and there she was, sitting on a wall, her head in her hands, and I felt so sorry for her. Because whatever else the rest of us got into – whatever mistakes the rest of us made – failing a course, or going out with the wrong girl, or joining a stupid club of posh twats, none of us were going to have to live with those mistakes for the rest of our lives, and it wasn't fair that she wasn't as free as us.

We were the only ones in the car park and if I'd been sober it would have been fine. I'd have been able to ask if she was OK. I could've just been the friend she needed. But I wasn't sober. And I wasn't the friend she needed. I was her ex-boyfriend – her stupid, drunk, self-pitying, selfish ex-boyfriend. The boyfriend of Lucy. But I wasn't thinking about Lucy at all. I wasn't even thinking about Karen. Just myself.

'You OK?' I said, sitting next to her.

'No.' She sniffed. She looked up. 'You shouldn't be here. Jonny wouldn't like it.'

'Jonny's a knob,' I said.

'Yeah. He is.'

And that was our big conversation. That's how well I listened to her. And then we were kissing, and I don't know what she was thinking but I wasn't thinking anything beyond how nice it felt, and how comfortable it was to be back with Karen again, feeling normal, feeling ordinary. I wasn't so much kissing her as remembering the life that I missed, and the more I kissed her, the more I missed it. I knew that Karen wasn't mine, that I was trying to relive something that was dead, but we kissed and when she asked me if I wanted to go somewhere with her I knew what she meant, but I wasn't saying no, even though my brain was trying to scream it over the boozy haze inside my skull. I was walking off with her towards her house, scowling at the unfairness of everything, absolutely determined to fuck everything up once and for all.

29. Charlotte

I'd need a wig, probably. Maybe a hat would do? I began scrolling through YouTube tutorials. *Drag moustache. Ultimate beard.*

A message flashed up on the screen.

> **Lucy:** Hiya. Whatchdoin?

> **Me:** Spanish homework. You?

> **Lucy:** Nothing ... I think Drew's going off me.

I felt my breath catching, just slightly.

> **Me:** What? No he isn't. Why would you say that?

> **Lucy:** He was really cagey about the party he's going to tonight. I asked him if I could come and I could tell he wasn't keen.

> **Me:** His friend's party? It's probably in Greenwood. He's embarrassed, or he thinks you'd be embarrassed.

> **Lucy:** Well that's another thing. He never wants me to meet his family. He's met my mum and dad, but I'm not allowed to meet his?

> **Me:** Same thing though. You saw that he felt

bad about not being able to go on the trip. It can't be easy for him.

Lucy: But I'm his girlfriend! If he can't be himself with me then what's the point? And he won't even sleep with me.

Me: Have you asked him about it?

Lucy: About the sex?

Me: Both.

Lucy: He says he wants to wait to make sure it's right. And he won't talk about where he lives.

Me: Well that's good isn't it? About wanting to wait?

Lucy: I get offers all the time you know. Maybe I should tell him that?

Me: I don't think you should. And you know those scuzzball rugby guys will shag anyone.

Lucy: Oh, thanks!!

Me: NOT WHAT I MEANT.

Lucy: LOL don't worry I know what you mean.

Me: Don't let this party thing get in your head. He's lucky to have you, and I bet he knows that. He'll have a crap time at the party and end up wishing he was out somewhere with you.

Lucy: OK. Thanks Char. Love you.

Me: Love you too babe. x

30. Drew

Sometimes you screw things up so badly that you don't know what to worry about first. When I woke up beside Karen, in her bed, both of us partially naked, my instinct was to cry. But I didn't have time for that. She was sleeping beside me, small and crumpled on the edge of the bed. I covered her with the duvet. Shit, shit, *shit*. This was very, very bad. I looked around the room – same room that I'd been in so often before. Nothing different. Same pink wallpaper that she must've had from being a little kid. Boy-band posters on the wall. The only different thing was her Tesco uniform hanging on the wardrobe door. A weirdly adult-looking thing in this room that looked as though it might be for a wee one. And what were we, lying in the middle of it? Children? Adults?

My stomach heaved. I grabbed a glass of water on the bedside table and downed it. It was stale. My head was thumping, ears vibrating the way they do when you leave a club. I could hear the blood pulsing around my brain. Why had I done this? All of the people that this would hurt came crashing into my thoughts at once. Lucy. Jonny. Mum. Charlotte. And what about Karen herself? Had I fucked up her whole marriage? Would her kid not have a dad now? How could a few tins of beer have kept me from thinking of all the hundreds of ways that sleeping with Karen would be a colossally bad idea?

'Jonny?' she muttered, stirring slightly.

'Ssshhh,' I said.

Oh God, don't wake up. If she thinks I'm Jonny and I can get out of here without her seeing me then maybe it will be OK? Maybe she'll think it was, I dunno, all a bad dream? That's the kind of absolutely mad thought I was having. As if it had been Karen, and not me, who was trolleyed last night. *No, you doofus, your pregnant ex-girlfriend was sober, wasn't she? She's highly frickin' unlikely to forget what happened.*

I, on the other hand, was scrambling around the mass of moments in my brain trying to piece it together. I could remember the lads telling me to leave it. The corridor. I remembered seeing Karen crying. Then it was a bit blurry ... I remembered walking off with her ... I remembered someone at the fire door having a fag. Who? *Try to remember. Please don't let it be someone who knew me ... The singer from the band maybe? God I hope so.*

'Oh SHIT!' Karen was awake and sitting bolt upright, staring at me like she'd woken up to find someone burgling her house. She was clutching the duvet to her chest. Her lipstick was smudged. Her mouth was stuttering to find words.

'I know! I know!' I said, running my hands through my hair.

It was all I could say. Both of us knew how bad this was. I was pulling on my clothes. The sooner I could get out, the sooner we could pretend that this had never happened. Shoes. Where were my feckin' shoes?

Karen was starting to lose it. She had her face in her hands and she was making these little noises that made her sound like an injured puppy.

'Drew, wait!' she cried as I made for the door.

I turned around.

'You can't just leave! We have to talk about this!'

No chance. I shook my head violently. 'It was an accident, Karen. I was drunk. We can't tell *anyone*. Let's just forget about it, OK?'

Her eyes were wide. Her mouth gaped open.

'Are you insane?' she said. 'We slept together!'

'Ssshhh!'

There was nobody home, I was sure of it, but all the same. Saying things out loud was dangerous. We absolutely could not talk about this. It would make it more real. What we needed right now was to forget …

'Drew!' she whispered urgently. 'We *did it*. Jonny's gonna kill me. He's gonna kill *you*!'

I sat down on her bed again, positioning myself in front of her. She was panicking and I had to take things in hand.

'Karen,' I said, the way you'd talk to a little kid who was spiralling into a tantrum, 'we did a wrong thing. A very wrong thing. I was drunk …'

'I wasn't, though!' she cried.

'But you are pregnant. And I don't want this to sound sexist, but it's bound to mess with your head a bit, right? Cos of hormones and everything? And you'd had a fight with Jonny. You didn't know what you were doing, right?'

She nodded, but I could tell she wasn't buying it, and to be honest neither was I. I'd known what I was doing as well. A thousand times I'd been drunk before and I'd never so much as kissed a girl by accident. All the booze did was give you a bit more confidence. All it did was help you ignore the part of your brain that was begging you not to make a big mistake. This was useless, but we had to try.

'If anyone found out about this, you know the conse-
quences would be really bad, right?' I was holding her
hand now.

She nodded again, tears splashing off her chin onto the
duvet.

'Nobody saw us. Nobody knows. Tell Jonny you went
home. I'll tell Dale I did the same.'

'They'll know,' she sobbed.

'They won't,' I said, not completely convinced myself.
'Know how I know?'

'How?'

'Because they know we're not that stupid. They know
we wouldn't risk all the good things in our lives.'

'But ... we did.'

'And that's our secret, Karen. That's our secret for the
rest of our whole lives, OK? Promise?'

She nodded. It was going to have to be enough. She
wiped her eyes with the duvet.

'You OK?' I said.

'No.'

'Me neither. But we will be. We can't let a mistake ruin
our lives, can we?'

'No,' she said, sniffing.

'I'm going now, but on Monday morning I'm going to
walk to school, and I'll just happen to bump into you on
the way to work, OK? And that way I can make sure you're
all right. It will all be over by then. You'll have made up
with Jonny. And what happened will be in the past.'

I offered a pathetic attempt at a smile and she tried to
smile back. I found my shoes on the stairs – one near the
bottom and one near the top. I wondered if her mum had
noticed. We must have been asleep by the time she'd got

back from the party. It was easy to sneak out the front door without being seen. Karen's kitchen backed into an entry that was always deserted. Once you were in it, it was only a few metres to the main walkway and out into the estate. I'd snuck out of her house a hundred times before.

Walking down the entry I felt the same shiver of energy I used to get after a night spent in her room when her mum was out. But it used to be a good feeling – a surge of something like triumph or joy. Now it was more like a ghost was walking beside me, tracing my spine with the cold finger of the past.

31. Charlotte

I looked at the wig in its plastic wrapper. I'd ordered it two days ago. It had come this morning and Mum wanted to know what it was.

'New top,' I said. 'Just a wee thing. Nothing expensive.'

She'd rolled her eyes and I ran upstairs to rip open the package. But now it was lying on my bed, still in the wrapper, and I honestly felt a bit afraid of it. I didn't know how to put on a wig. Where do you put your own hair? On YouTube the videos I'd seen were mostly men with short hair putting on long wigs – women's hairstyles. What if it slipped off? The YouTube tutorials had said to buy a lace fronted one so I did, but I didn't know how to trim it properly. What if I tried to do it and I did it wrong and ruined it? Maybe Jay could help. Maybe he'd laugh at me. But why would he? Still, it felt so silly and childish. To want to dress up. I hadn't done it since I was in primary school. The last time was probably wanting to dress as Batman and my mum wouldn't let me so I had to be Batgirl as a compromise. She'd wanted me to be a fairy princess.

I tipped the wig out onto the bed and touched it. It was black and slightly puffy – Elvis style, a bouffant with sideburns, but more subtle than the Elvis wigs you see on Halloween. The hair was soft. I suddenly wondered if it was real hair and dropped it. But that was silly. It was synthetic – I knew that.

I went to the door and opened it a crack. I could hear Mum downstairs clattering plates, probably on the verge of ordering takeout. She had her music on. I heard the pop of a Prosecco cork. Yep, definitely takeout tonight. I closed the door. She'd be busy for a few minutes, but I put my bag behind the door just in case. It would give me a second to pull the wig off if she suddenly came in.

I sat at my dressing table and tied my hair back from my face. *Goodbye, Charlotte.* I pulled the wig on and adjusted it. The lace hung in front of my eyes but I could see through it. I twisted my mouth into an Elvis sneer. *Uh-huh-huh.* I touched the soft sideburns, letting my hand follow down my chin line. So smooth. What would it be like to have that rough sandpaper on your face? Would it make you feel less vulnerable? Could I fight someone? I closed my eyes and imagined myself as a man, as big as Adam, bigger, with my fists clenched.

Mum called and I pulled the wig off and shoved it in my drawer. She'd had her fairy princess for long enough. It was time for a new costume.

32. Drew

She was so jumpy – the way she started when she saw me. Like she'd been waiting for death and finally here I was.

'Hiya,' I said, trying to seem light and breezy.

'All right?' Karen said, looking like doom.

We walked towards Tesco.

'So?' I said. 'How is everything?'

She knew what I meant. I meant *How is Jonny? Does anyone know? Are we safe?*

'OK. I think,' she said.

'You think?'

That pissed her off.

'Well, it's pretty flippin' hard keeping this from your fiancé, you know!' she hissed. 'We don't have secrets from each other. Not normally. I feel terrible about it, Drew!'

'You can't tell him,' I said. The breeziness had lasted for all of about twenty seconds.

'Shut up. I'm not going to,' she said.

'Good. So it's OK then. He doesn't know. Nobody knows. It's cool.'

'It's not cool!'

'Ssshhh. Tell the street why don't you!'

'Sorry.' She lowered her voice. 'But it's not in any way cool. Not even slightly. We'll have to live with this for the rest of our lives, Drew.'

I wanted to tell her not to be so dramatic. That accidents happened. That there was no need to blow this all out of proportion. But the truth was I felt bad about it too. Jonny wasn't my best mate, but he was a mate. Dale and I had always made fun of him a bit – slaggin' him when he was trying to be serious about something. He hadn't deserved any of that, but sleeping with his pregnant girl-friend felt like the worst sort of bullying.

'Did you make it up with Jonny then?'

'What?'

'The argument. At the wedding. Did yous make it up?'

'Oh. Yeah. It wasn't a big deal, really. He came over and brought me flowers. So I spent Sunday crying because he'd been so nice.'

'I'm sorry,' I said.

'My own fault,' she said.

'It was mine too.'

'You're not the engaged one.'

'Yeah, but you were upset. I shouldn't have gone out after you. I just wasn't really thinking. I'm really sorry, Karen.'

'I know.'

We were at the gates of the supermarket. She shrugged and then stuck out her hand. It was weird and formal, but I shook it, because what else were we going to do?

'Friends?' she said.

'Yeah,' I said. 'Thanks.'

'See you around, Drew.'

'See ya.'

And I wish that had been the end of the whole thing. I really do. But it wasn't. And even walking to school I must have known somehow that you can't just do a thing like that and get away with it. People like Adam might get away with something like that, but ordinary people don't.

The first indication I had that something was wrong was a text that came through just as I reached the school grounds. Dale. He hadn't messaged me after the party and I thought that was weird because I'd just bailed. I'd disappeared. At the very least I'd expected him to ask me where I'd got to. But nothing. Not even an update on Instagram about his evening and how drunk everyone had been. No candid pictures of Dale making an idiot of himself on the dance floor. He'd gone dark.

I'd messaged him on Sunday night:

> What's the craic? Sore head?

And the reply he sent as I reached school:

> Yeah.

That was it. *Yeah.* So something was up. I wasn't going to assume the worst. Not yet. I was going to be logical. He was probably upset because I'd left the party and hadn't gone back. So I texted him again.

> I'm sorry about leaving the party. I was sooo drunk. Almost passed out in the car park! I just went home.

The reply came swiftly.

> NP

NP? He couldn't even be bothered writing out *No problem* in full?

That was the first indication that everything was not OK. The second came after first period, Spanish.

It was Monday morning. Nobody's on top form on Monday morning. You could put a lot of bad feeling down to that. I had only just begun to get over my hangover and the sweeping paranoia that went with it, complicated by my guilt. I told myself that everyone else seeming a bit 'off' was partly an extension of the hangover, and partly just everyone else's Monday blues. Spanish class seemed to drag on for ever. Don Antonio kept running his hand through his hair like he was trying to solve a big puzzle rather than putting us through vocab lists. I looked across to Charlotte hoping to make a face or roll my eyes – something humorous to show I was losing the will to live. But she wasn't even looking up. Her hair fell over her face, which was glued to her book, but you could tell she wasn't concentrating because she wasn't turning the pages in time with Don Antonio and the rest of the class.

At break I went down to the lockers to get my stuff for the next class and Artie was there, standing with his back to the metal boxes, arms folded, one leg bent at the knee, foot on the locker.

'All right?' I said, approaching him. He was right beside my locker. If I'd opened it, it would have opened right into his face. I was expecting him to move. But he didn't. He didn't even look at me.

'Artie?' I said, thinking that maybe he hadn't heard me.

He put his foot back on the floor and turned his whole body to face me, looked me right in the eyes and said, 'We need to talk.'

'Oh, OK,' I said. 'Sounds serious?'

He wasn't smiling. In fact he looked angry, and he didn't reply. He just walked off and I guessed that he wanted me to follow him. We went outside and he walked right across the football field to the other side, not far from the Stewards' club house. There was nobody about. The sky was dark and it was cold. Most people had stayed in the cafeteria.

I blew on my hands to make them warmer. 'It's freezing, Artie. What's this about?'

'You're cold all right,' he said, spinning around, accusing me.

'I know,' I said, not getting it. 'It's Baltic.'

'No.' He rolled his eyes. 'You're *cold*. You're a cold person. A cold-hearted asshole.'

'Oh. What?'

How could he know? Please let this be about something else ... But I knew it wasn't. I had seconds to decide how to play it. Deny everything? Full remorse? Why hadn't I made a plan?

'You *know* what,' he hissed. 'You slept with some girl. At that party the other night. Didn't you?'

The force of the accusation was like a punch in the stomach. I could barely breathe. My brain scrambled for something to say, something to get me off the hook, anything to make me seem sympathetic. But instead I heard myself saying 'How did you know?' and even as the words came out I knew that they shouldn't because it wasn't a question, it was an admission, and even Artie looked surprised that I'd said it so eagerly.

I noticed that his fists were clenched. I didn't say anything else because I was afraid of what might come out. Such an idiot. Why did I admit to everything straight away?

'I had a date the other night,' he said.

It seemed like such a weird thing to say that for a second I wondered if he was changing the subject. I wasn't sure how to respond but he was looking at me, waiting for me to say something.

'Right. Em, how did it go?'

'It went great, asshole,' he said.

I felt angry then. I felt like punching him. I knew he was right. I *was* an asshole. But I didn't like hearing it. And I had no response, again, but it didn't matter because he started to tell me the whole story. It all came pouring out.

'I was showing Crispy my pics,' he said.

I fought the urge to laugh at his name. Crispy. What kind of crap name was that?

'We were scrolling through and I was pointing out my friends, Charlotte and Lucy – you remember, your *girlfriend Lucy* – and you.'

Jeez, he was really going for it with the guilt. I wished he'd get to the point.

'Crispy said he liked your shirt in the picture. I remember that, because I felt a bit jealous. Anyway, I told him about the four of us, about how we go to Buster's and about the poetry slam and everything. I told him how you and Lucy were such a nice couple.'

His eyes were narrow. He was doing his very best to make me feel the very worst.

'And then, just yesterday, I got this text from him. Would you like me to read it?'

Not really, I thought. But I knew he was going to read it whatever my response. He took his time locating it, just to add to my suffering. I wondered if the break bell had gone. Was I going to be late to class?

'Ah, here it is: *Hi Artie. Guess what? Last night the band were playing this scuzzy community centre engagement party for some pregnant teen chav ...*'

Shit. He was in the band. And Dale had been right – he *had* been looking down on us.

'Hey,' I said, my face starting to get hot. 'You can have a go at me, but not her. It's not her fault, OK? And it's not scuzzy. We're not all as rich as you.'

'Oh sorreee. Didn't mean to offend your bit on the side.'

It was my turn to clench my fists. *Keep it cool, Drew.* I knew I was in the wrong, but he had no right to talk about Karen like she was some kind of slapper. I tried to breathe deeply and I let him continue.

'... *It was all going well until she had a proper meltdown with her beloved fiancé,*' he went on. '*OMG I thought she was going to swing for him. Anyway. She storms out, right in the middle of our set, and this guy goes after her – not her fiancé, some other guy ...*' Artie looked up at me. 'Sound familiar, Drew?'

I couldn't speak.

'... *So after the song I went out for a smoke and there they were – the two of them sucking the faces off each other ...*'

He looked up at me again. Was he hoping for a reaction? A denial?

'How romantic, Drew. The run-down community-centre car park.'

There it was again, that sneering tone. I knew he was doing it because he was angry, but it wasn't fair. He'd probably gone to some fancy restaurant on his date with 'Crispy'. It was wrong that I'd kissed Karen, but it hadn't been this horrible sordid thing that he was describing. I'd just felt sorry for her, that was all. The kiss was like a comfort-memory or something – something we used to do to make ourselves feel better – and it seemed natural at the time, even though it seemed wrong as well. I could never explain it, especially not to Artie, and I'd just have to stand there and take the lumps and hope that it was over soon. I closed my eyes. He carried on.

'... *So then they left, no doubt off to find a place for a shag, and bloody hell, as they walked past I recognised him. From your photo. That boy with the nice shirt. I know it was him because he was wearing the exact same shirt. It was definitely him. Didn't you say he was going out with your other friend?*'

Artie snapped his phone case shut, folded his arms and just stood there, staring at me with his head tipped to one side, looking disgusted.

'It was a mistake,' I started.

He snorted with laughter. 'Oh, *too right* it was a mistake.'

'Look,' I said, deadly serious, 'it really was a mistake. I was drunk. It was a massive, stupid, idiotic mistake. I really regret it, Artie. I don't want to hurt Lucy, and I don't think you want to hurt her either.'

'Oh, what? Don't try to make this my fault,' he said.

His voice was raised and I glanced about. Still nobody nearby.

'Sorry,' I said. 'I didn't mean to make it sound like that. Obviously you can tell her if you like, but I swear this won't happen again. The girl I was with – she wasn't just anyone – she's my ex, and –'

'That makes it WORSE if anything,' spat Artie.

'I know, I'm just trying to explain. I felt sorry for her, and –'

'You felt horny, more like.'

'That too, I suppose. I know it was wrong. Just ... please don't tell Lucy? She doesn't deserve to get hurt, and I truly won't do it again. I won't.'

He was shaking his head and then he took two steps towards me so that his face was really close to mine. 'Lucy is one of the best people in this school. You have NO idea how lucky you are to have her. You don't deserve her.'

There was so much anger in his voice that I felt like crying. He was right. I didn't deserve Lucy. Or any of these chances I'd been given. I was just a stupid kid from a council estate and I didn't deserve any of this.

He stepped back and took an audible breath, standing up straight as if he was composing himself. Maybe he was trying to stop himself from hitting me.

'I'm not going to tell her,' he said finally.

'Thank you,' I whispered.

'I'm not doing it for *you*.'

'I understand.'

He jabbed his finger towards me. 'If you *ever* do this again ...'

'I won't,' I said. I meant it. I never would. I never meant to in the first place, but now I knew what it felt like to have done it, I knew I wouldn't do it again. 'I swear to God I won't.'

'Good.'

He said it like that was the final word on the matter. But there was something else I needed to say. How could I ask him for anything? But I had to. He turned to leave.

'Wait,' I said.

He turned around, silent, stone-faced.

'Artie. Are you going to tell Charlotte?'

He rolled his eyes. 'Telling Charlotte would be the same thing as telling Lucy,' he said. '*Some* people are loyal, Drew. You've made me a *bad friend* today. I should be telling Lucy, but I can't. And now here you are asking me not to tell Charlotte?'

'I'm so sorry. I just need to know what to expect.'

'Charlotte has enough on her plate right now without the stress of this.'

And then he turned and strode off back to school and left me standing there by the clubhouse, wondering what he meant.

33. Charlotte

'Stand up straight,' he said. 'No. *Straight.*'

Jay got up from the table and stood behind me on the stage. He put one hand on my shoulder and another on my bum. 'Excuse my hands, but needs must.'

He gave my bum a shove forward, holding my shoulder where it was. 'There. And chin *up*.' His voice rose on 'up'. I could feel what he was saying. It was different.

'You see?' he said, as if he could read my mind. 'Now, legs slightly apart, as if you've got a ... well, you know. Yes, that's it. Oh my. *That's* the stance you're looking for. I'll take a picture so you can see ...'

Buster's was closed and Portia had allowed us to use it for a lesson. He was teaching me how to be a man. Or at least, a girl in man-drag.

'What's up with you, gurl? You look like shit.'

It made me smile. 'Oh, thanks so much,' I said.

'Got you smiling anyway.'

He was right. My heart wasn't in it. I'd wanted to know how to create a character, so I could be as bold as I needed to be. But I didn't feel like playing around today. I wanted to hide. Not to stand on a stage. The final round of the slam was in a couple of days.

'Seriously, though, what's up?'

I wasn't about to get into it with him. I shrugged. 'I don't know if I really want to do this after all,' I said. 'It's harder than I thought.'

Jay rolled his eyes. 'Everyone thinks drag is just about dressing up. I told you before, it's more than that.'

'I know,' I said, sitting down on the stage. 'I suppose I'm just tired right now.'

'Tired?' he said, crossing his legs. 'Is this boy trouble?'

How did he know?

Again, he went on as if he knew everything. 'Cos boy trouble might be the thing you need right now.'

I seriously doubted it. Not the kind of trouble I had.

I shook my head, but I felt curious. 'What do you mean?'

'Well. The boy who's causing you trouble. He's an asshole, right? I mean, even if you love him, he's tearing you up, so he's an asshole. Am I right?'

I nodded. One hundred per cent.

'So you become him.'

'What?' I didn't want to become Adam. I couldn't want anything less than I wanted that.

'I mean you channel that Asshole Man Energy. Whatever it is – that's your character. You critique the *shit* out of that guy by becoming him. Think about it – you can say whatever you like, be whatever you like, have him say and do your bidding. You don't always have to be lovely, you know.'

He was walking around now, gripping his belt and wading around the empty café, bow-legged like a cowboy, head thrown back, smoking an imaginary cigarette.

'I'm king of this here café,' he said. 'An' I can get any gal I like,' he pointed at me, 'just by looking in her sweet face and turnin' on ma charm.' On the word 'charm' he grabbed his crotch.

He winked at me before becoming himself again, seeming to physically shrink as he dropped his shoulders and walked back to his seat.

I got it then. Jay was a guy, but not like that.

'That was amazing,' I said.

'Charlotte, we get told all the time that the world is a stage.' He was suddenly serious, leaning forward, wanting me to hear this. 'But if you're a performer then that little spot up there –' He pointed to the small raised rectangle with the single mic. 'That's your world. And you can call anyone out, say anything, be anyone. Just be smart about it. Make it real.'

I walked home with those words bouncing around in my head. For the first time since the start of term I was feeling hopeful, as if I could have something completely for myself. What if I said everything, *really everything*, but not as myself? It wouldn't make my problem with Adam go away, I knew that. But I felt like hugging myself as I reached our street, because it was a way to grab a thread of this whole horrific tangle that I couldn't unravel. In the real world Adam had everything – every way of owning things belonged to him, and I hated him for it. But maybe I could own my own world, somehow? Fight back, even if it was just within myself? Maybe it would be a start?

I pulled the door shut and Mum called from the kitchen. 'How was study?'

'Great!' I said, trying not to sound too suspiciously upbeat. 'I mean, it was hard, but good too.'

'OK,' she called back.

If she had any idea what I was planning I'd never be allowed to leave the house again.

34. Drew

I saw Dale as I turned out of the estate on my way to school. He was ahead of me, probably walking to work. I knew I had to ask him.

'Dale!' I called.

He didn't turn round.

'*Dale!*'

Again, no response.

I wasn't going to shout again. Kids were starting to stare. But I was sure he hadn't heard me. So I picked up speed to catch up and I nudged into him.

'Hey, watch it,' he said, straight-faced.

I'd been right. Something *was* wrong.

'*Dale!*'

He stopped and turned towards me. 'What? What do you want, Drew?'

I shrugged. 'What's the craic? Are you angry cos I didn't go back to the party that night?'

He did this little fake laugh and started walking on. I couldn't leave it there.

'Dale, please. Just stop for one sec,' I said, now breathless because he was walking double speed, the way he always did.

And he did stop. I was going to be late for school, but I didn't care. I had to make him level with me. 'Tell me what this is all about,' I said.

'OK, fine,' said Dale.

And then he told me.

'You slept with Karen that night, didn't you?'

I looked at his face for clues about how I should react but there was nothing, just a stony, silent frown.

'I just ...' I started. But I couldn't finish it.

'Save it,' he said. 'You left that party with her and never came back, and neither did she. You're gutted about her marrying Jonny and having his kid, even though you split up last year. The whole night at that party you couldn't stop looking at her.'

'That's not true,' I said.

I'd looked at her a couple of times. She was looking good, that was true. But I was happy for her and Jonny. Wasn't I?

'What's not true?' Dale said. 'That you weren't looking at her, or that you didn't sleep with her?'

There was no point in lying to him. He'd never trust me again if I did. I couldn't say the words, though. I just looked at the ground and started thinking about jumping out in front of the next bus that came past.

'I knew it,' he said.

I looked up then, and there was something else in his face besides rage. Disgust, maybe.

'It was a big mistake,' I said.

He nodded. 'Yeah.'

He started walking on.

'Wait!' I called, but he wasn't waiting.

I knew there was no point in trying to catch him up and making him late for work, giving him another reason to hate me. But I had to do something because I couldn't spend all day wondering whether he was going to tell Jonny, wondering whether I'd have a friend in the world by the end of the day.

I walked the rest of the way to school with a tightness in my chest that I couldn't shift. It made me want to bend over and catch my breath, but I was late already. What could I do? I couldn't text Dale because then he'd have written proof of what I'd done. I couldn't call him because he was at work. I would have to try not to think about it until after school and then try to call by the garage as he was getting out.

But that wasn't the only thing that happened that day to make me realise how unsafe my secret was.

Just after break I was in the sixth-form centre. At first I'd been glad that it was quiet and especially that Charlotte and Artie weren't there. That little first-year kid who'd been following me around had brought me more Coke at break time, plus a packet of Kit Kats for some reason, and I was going to sit in the centre, have a drink and have a look at the new Lorca poem Don Antonio had given us that morning. It was a poem about forbidden love. *Thanks, Lorca, just what I need right now*, I thought.

I sat down near the wall at one end of the centre. I'd rather have been sitting near the window, letting the strong sun toast me through the glass, but I needed to lie low for a bit. It was hard to concentrate on the poem. I had upset so many people. I was trying to think of something to say to Dale to make him realise that I really meant that I was sorry, that I really had made a mistake, and that's when Adam came in.

'Drew!' he cried, far too loudly.

Great. This was all I needed. Steward 'banter'. No doubt he'd want to talk about Jamesy's party. I really was not in the mood.

'Oh, hi, Adam. I was just going to the library.'

I started to get up but he sat down opposite me and waved me to sit again. And I did it. Adam was one of those people who have a kind of gravitational pull that makes you compelled to follow them, even when you don't want to.

'You can spare a minute for a fellow Steward, right?'

I smiled as genuinely as I could.

'So,' said Adam, leaning forward, a sly grin on his face. '*Someone*'s been a bit naughty!'

'Have they?' I said.

I wondered what he was going to tell me. I had heard that Charles's dad had almost caught on to his weed farm last week when he found a spliff in Charles's blazer pocket.

'Is it Charles?' I asked.

Adam looked confused for a second, then he broke out into his big grin again. 'No, you dope. It's *you*.'

Oh. This was not happening. *How?*

'You look a tad surprised,' said Adam. He was absolutely loving this. I tried to focus on breathing. I took a drink of Coke, trying to seem cool, undisturbed, but I choked on it slightly. Adam laughed.

'Don't worry,' he said, getting up to clap me on the back mid-cough. 'Your secret's safe with me. And I think we just found ourselves a bit of rent.'

I shook my head in surrender. 'How did you find out?'

Adam leaned back in his chair. 'I heard you and that little Artie guy you're always hanging around with.'

'How? There was nobody around?'

'Well, that's what you thought, clearly,' he said, raising an amused eyebrow. 'I was in the clubhouse. The window was open. I heard everything.'

'But ... there weren't any lights on,' I said pathetically. As if you could argue a thing into not having happened.

Adam shrugged. 'Sometimes I don't switch them on?'

My brain hurt. The rising number of People Who Knew had overtaken any hope I'd felt of this whole thing passing over. Dale, Artie, now Adam. And of course who knew if Karen herself would be able to keep everything quiet? My head was full of suggestions, none of them helpful. Should I just tell Lucy now? Should I confess to Jonny?

'Hey,' said Adam, in a tone that sounded almost friendly. 'Don't sweat it. These things happen. You dirty dawg!' He grinned again, the compassionate tone gone. 'Look, I'm not going to tell anyone. Just, maybe be more careful in future, eh? You don't want to ruin things with the lovely Lucy. Us *ladies men* have to maximise our chances to keep in the game, you know?'

I was going to be sick.

'Excuse me,' I managed to whisper as I ran to the loos.

I could hear him chuckling behind me. It was a joke to him. I wondered if he'd ever cared about anyone besides himself. When I got back to the sixth-form centre I was alone. Thank goodness, Adam had gone, and it was still twenty minutes until the bell. I wished I could make him permanently disappear. I hated him. I was afraid of him, but I was angry too. The way he talked about girls. The way he talked about Lucy. But was I any better? I was the one who'd cheated. I was the one who'd taken advantage of my pregnant ex-girlfriend. Betrayed my friend, my girlfriend. Maybe it was me who didn't care about anyone else.

The bell sounded. The noise of it was like lightning passing from one ear to the other through my skull.

I dragged myself to the classroom and sat down, trying not to look anyone in the face, especially not the teacher, especially not Charlotte. This lesson was going to suck on so many levels. I opened the iPad that was sitting, ready, on my desk and clicked on the relevant app. There was something new – a note labelled 'Granada Trip'. It was a letter to parents to tell students what to bring on the trip. There was a list of students at the top of the page, My name was on it.

My heart thumped inside me. Adam must have paid for it. The Stewards. I was going to Granada. I'd never been out of the country before, except to visit my uncle in Scotland, and for a second, a *split second*, a shiver of excitement rose up in my chest. But then I remembered everything else and the waves of nausea and guilt crashed over the thrill. I obviously couldn't go, could I? I couldn't let myself have this thing – this life that I wanted. Not when I knew what it would mean to Lucy. She wanted to sleep with me on that trip. I'd promised her. And I could never do that now, could I? Not after what I'd done. Maybe I'd never sleep with anyone ever again.

I closed the iPad case with a snap, and the room went quiet, and when I looked up everyone was looking at me and I realised that the lesson had started and Don Antonio had been reading about Lorca and everyone else was following the text on their iPads. Don Antonio was looking at me too.

'Everything OK, Andrew?' he asked.

'Um, yeah. Sorry. Lost my place.'

He nodded, unsmiling.

At the end of class as people were filing out, he caught my eye.

'A quick word?' he said gravely.

I hung back, trying not to notice Charlotte's sympathetic smile as she left with the others. I couldn't take much more of this absolute car-crash of a day. I'd keep quiet, agree with whatever he said, promise to work harder. I'd do whatever I could to leave as soon as possible. I took a deep breath as the door drew to a gentle close on the now-silent room.

Don Antonio beckoned me to his desk with a nod of the head and I took up a seat in front of him. We sat there for a few seconds and I wondered if he was expecting me to talk first. Or maybe it was just that he was thinking about what to say? Eventually he broke the silence with a deep sigh and a tap of his pen on the desk.

'Your work is suffering,' he said.

'I know,' I said. 'I'm sorry.'

'Is there something you need help with?'

He tone was odd. Not rude, but serious. I guessed that he'd had enough of the lazy new kid who couldn't be arsed doing the homework.

'No, I don't need help really,' I said.

But then something happened. It was on the word 'help'. Something inside me just broke a little bit. Like the tiniest of cracks in a glass full of water. I looked up at Don Antonio to see if he'd heard it in my voice, and his face had softened. He had. There was a hard lump in my throat making it difficult to say anything else but I had to. I couldn't sit there and break down in front of the teacher. Not today. Not any day.

He spoke before I was able. 'Like I said before, Andrew, Cooke's can be a tough place.'

I nodded, swallowing the lump, breathing out through my nose.

'I will catch everything up. I'll do it this weekend,' I said. I meant it too. That's what I needed now – to keep my head down and work.

'OK,' he said.

There was a pause. Don Antonio was looking at my blazer pocket. The Stewards badge.

'How's everything going. With the Stewards?' he asked.

I could've just said 'Fine'. I could have shrugged and said 'OK'. But I didn't. Instead I started to cry. You'd think it would be humiliating to cry in front of a teacher. To sit there sobbing at a desk with your head in your hands, in front of the person who gives you assignments. But by that stage I really didn't care. All I could think of was how good it felt to finally burst my insides like this in front of someone else. As if I'd been a bomb that had exploded after waiting and waiting and ticking away for so long. And he just sat there, Don Antonio. He didn't even say anything, or do anything, he just sat there and let me cry, for minutes that felt like for ever. And when it was coming to an end he held out the box of tissues from his desk and I took one and it was like a magic object that brought me back into the real world, because as I wiped my eyes I was suddenly thinking, *What next? How do you explain this one, Drew? Tell him everything? Anything?*

'I think I'm going to leave school,' I said.

It was blunt, but he didn't look shocked.

'And why is that?' he said.

I shrugged, trying to give myself time to think. A mistake.

He spoke again, pushing his fingertips together. 'Andrew, you can tell me anything, you know? But I need

162

to let you know that if you tell me anything about you being harmed or harming other people, I have to pass that on. OK?'

I knew what he meant. He meant physical abuse, or sexual abuse, or mental torture. Stuff like that. He didn't mean the harm I was doing by cheating on my girlfriend. But I didn't want to tell him. 'I'm just not enjoying it, sir. I mean, I know you're not actually meant to enjoy school, but ... this one ... it's so different to my old life.'

My *old* life? Just a few days ago I'd been at a party with my friends from Greenwood, and then in bed with Karen.

Don Antonio nodded. 'It's a culture shock to most people who come in from the outside,' he said.

'But the thing is,' I went on, 'my old friends ... they're not really my old friends. They're still my friends now. But they're not ...'

He nodded again, even though I wasn't making sense.

'I tell you what,' he said. The kindness that I'd noticed missing at the start of class had returned to his voice. 'Come on the trip with us. Come to Granada. Let's see if I can't persuade you that there aren't some good things about this school. Sí?'

'OK,' I said miserably.

'Try to hang in there. The first couple of months of a new place can be the worst.'

Months! The trip in March seemed like an eternity away. I couldn't possibly tell him about Lucy or Charlotte or Karen or anything else. I'd have to figure it all out myself. But maybe he was right. Maybe the trip was the place to do that. If I could lie low for a bit until then? There'd be exams, and then Christmas ... maybe it was possible.

Being away from home, having some space to think about my next move, seemed like a good idea. I'd be away from everyone who knew about me and Karen. No threat for at least a week if I could make it to March without Jonny finding out. It would give me some breathing space. That's what I needed.

For the rest of the day I kept my head down and tried to avoid everyone. It wasn't too difficult because I didn't have classes with Lucy or Artie or Charlotte. I spent lunchtime in the toilet fiddling around with my phone, wondering if I should text Dale, wondering what to say to him, worrying that he'd already called Karen or Jonny. By the time the last bell sounded I was convinced that everyone already knew. That my life was over, and that I might as well go to Granada and maybe just stay there and never come back.

As I walked in the direction of Dale's garage I fantasised about it. I mean, maybe it wasn't impossible? I could speak Spanish pretty well. I could doss around for a couple of weeks and look for work giving English lessons or something? I wasn't qualified, obviously, but I wouldn't need a proper job – just something for a few quid every now and again. It would be sunny – I wouldn't even really need a place to stay for a while.

It was stupid, I knew that, but the thought of potentially just quitting everything and stepping on a plane and never coming back was so comforting. Even if I would never have had the guts to do it, just the fact that you *could*, technically, do something like that made it possible to imagine being alive after this whole thing came out. And I was convinced that it would all come out.

I waited for Dale on the wall near the garage and, sure enough, after a half hour or so he came past. He'd been bobbing along, the way he always does, like he's on springs, but when he saw me he slowed down. It was like I'd turned the wind off and pulled him back to earth.

'What now?' he asked, scowling.

'Dale,' I said, getting up and joining him on the walk towards our estate.

He sped up again and I was practically running to keep up.

'Look, I deserve everything. I know that. I deserve for everyone to find out. I just –'

'You want me to say I won't tell Jonny and Karen,' he said, eyes forward, not even glancing my direction.

I felt like a piece of dirt.

'Yes,' I said.

He stopped then and faced me, almost laughing as he shook his head. 'You're actually unbelievable,' he said.

I hung my head.

'You think that I'm such a crap friend to Karen and Jonny that I'm going to ruin their relationship over this?'

I looked up. He was shaking his head.

'You're so *selfish*,' he said, spitting out the word like it was the worst insult. 'As if I'd tell them! She's pregnant, Drew. They're engaged. Of course I'm not going to tell them. And you'd better not bloody do it either, right? I mean, if our friendship means anything to you, that is.'

His voice cracked a bit and that's when I realised that it wasn't just anger. I had betrayed our group. I'd ruined everything. Dale had been my best friend and I'd put him in this horrible position where he knew something and couldn't tell. I'd hurt *everyone*.

'I'm so sorry, Dale,' I said, wiping my eyes. 'It won't ever happen again. I know you don't want to be my friend any more,' I said. Another deep breath. 'But I hope that someday you will forgive me for messing everything up so much.' He still wasn't looking at me. I had to hope that he was listening. 'And if that day comes then please let me know because, I swear, there won't be a day when I don't wake up regretting how this cost me my best friend.'

He wiped at his eye. He had been listening. It was all I was going to get. He walked off towards his house without a word and I gulped the air and ran towards my own.

35. Charlotte

I applied the moustache as Jay had shown me. Smoothed
it down and wiggled my nose to make sure it would stay.
Mum was out. Artie's friend was picking me up in an hour.
Jet black hair, styled by Jay so that it was slightly less Elvis,
black eyeliner. The moustache was the last thing. I hardly
recognised myself. But then I looked at my poem and there
I was again. One last practice before I left. I stood, two
feet away from the full-length mirror, and took the stance:
feet slightly apart, shoulders back, head high – chin
tipped slightly forward. I looked myself dead in the eyes.
Carpe diem.

> Who do you think you're looking at?
>
> Let me explain myself
>
> I am your best hope of passing
>
> I am your best man
>
> But don't be afraid
>
> I'm your biggest fan
>
> I will write you letters
>
> On the backs of envelopes
>
> From the STI clinic
>
> You think it's funny?
>
> Well what's a guy supposed to do
>
> When you wear those come-here-kiss-me
> shoes?

Come on

I can't help it.

And you know that neither can you.

And that's the thing:

It's natural, right?

We're top of the game

Meant to be together

Meant to bang, whatever

You feel.

Sorry

Was that rude?

Well, good.

Cos now you know the truth

I'm not just your dream

The captain of the rugby team

The one that everyone wants to be seen with

I'm not just the number one

Not just the privileged son

Not just the strength and pride of my tight

little unit

And I know that you want it

And you know it

But I'm a liar too

And I'll make a slut out of you

If I want to

All it takes is one word

Yes, you heard,

I could turn this all around

In a heartbeat

I'll go from

Offering you a seat

To removing your chair

I'll see you lying there

Wondering how you fell

Wondering if you should tell

Should you mention it?

Well

Just think about whose pocket they're in

Where would you begin?

You

Cannot

Win

36. Drew

I ran away from Dale, into my own house, into the kitchen. The washing machine was on. I could hear Mum hoovering in the living room. Good. I ran upstairs, threw myself on the bed, face in the pillow, and cried myself to sleep.

When I woke up it was 10.30 p.m. No hoover. House completely quiet. There was a note tucked under the door.

> Didn't want to wake you love. Your dinner's
> in the fridge.

They must have gone to bed. I stumbled downstairs, my head banging like a Lambeg drum. I filled a glass of water and the coldness of it stung my throat but it felt so good. I refilled the glass and downed it. I looked at my phone. Three missed calls and three messages, all from Lucy.

> Hi Drew. I'm at Buster's. Have you remem-
> bered about the poetry slam final tonight?

Oh no. I had not remembered! How could I have forgotten? I read the other messages.

> It's started. We've saved you a seat. Hope
> you're on the way!

Then:

> Drew! Charlotte's about to go on! You're
> going to miss her poem!

That message had only been sent a couple of minutes ago. It was too late now. I looked at my phone. The bus would leave in ten minutes. I was still in my school uniform. I hadn't eaten. I was starving and groggy and I probably smelt disgusting. I could do it though – ten minutes? I could just about do it. I owed it to Lucy, and to Charlotte. I'd missed her performance but I could see her at least. I could try.

I took my keys and wallet from my blazer, grabbed my jacket and ran out of the house. As I reached the stop at the edge of the estate I could see the bus pulling into our road. Breathless, I got on and showed the driver my ticket. He nodded and I flung myself into a seat. I was sweaty. I knew I looked like hell, but the run had woken me up properly and I was beginning to feel good about just doing something. Even though it wasn't much – even though I'd messed up the evening – at least I was moving, going somewhere. Time to contact Lucy.

> Lucy! I'm so sorry! I fell asleep and only just woke up. On the bus now!

None of it was a lie. I just left out the part about completely forgetting about the slam. My heart jumped when she texted back.

> You missed her. She was amazing.

Crap. I had really wanted to see her.

> I'm sooo sorry!! Is the whole thing over?? Did anyone film it?

Lucy wrote:

> Three poets still to go. I took a video of Charlotte.

It was impossible to tell how angry she was. Maybe she wasn't being her usual chatty self because other people were performing? *Face it, Drew, she is really, really pissed off.*

See you in a few minutes

I deserved it if she was cold towards me. I deserved everything. I stared out of the bus window at the quiet, dark houses, wondering why the hell I hadn't just stayed in bed. It didn't help that my stomach was starting to growl. The shop at the bus station wouldn't even be open to grab a packet of crisps. Getting off the bus, the rain started spitting, so I picked up my pace and started jogging towards Buster's. School looked so different in the dark. The empty car park looked like a mouth opening at the entrance to the building. Everything was much bigger in the silence. The jog turned into a run as the drops of rain multiplied. Buster's was glowing from the outside. It was packed. I could almost feel my wet jacket starting to steam before I'd reached the door. I was glad it was busy. Maybe nobody would notice me coming in late.

I opened the door carefully, trying not to disturb the poet who I could see was mid-flow. I scanned the room. Artie was at our usual table, his arm around a guy. Not the singer from the party, though, someone else. And Lucy was at the table too, but not Charlotte. I looked around but I couldn't see her. I waited until the poet had finished a noisy rhythmic rant about online dating. The room was going wild, people standing up, clapping, cheering.

I bumped and apologised my way to the table and I was about to tap Lucy on the shoulder when the guy with Artie turned around and our eyes met, and I knew his eyes, and it took me a minute to figure it out, but then I did figure it out, and I forgot that I was meant to be feeling embarrassed and regretful and instead I shouted, 'Holy *shit*, Charlotte!' because it was Charlotte – she was Artie's man – dressed in beige chinos, a smart pinstripe shirt and tie, and she had a moustache and a goatee that looked so *real*, and, 'Oh my God, you look amazing!' I said. She was laughing and then she said, this man, smiling, with Charlotte's mouth, 'Sit down, you knob. Why are you wearing your uniform?'

37. Charlotte

I was the only one laughing when he clocked that it was me. You should have seen his face! It was brilliant. But it was also really obvious that nobody else was amused. Lucy was scowling and Artie was looking the other way, as if he hadn't noticed. I stopped laughing and we sat down. Drew could see that I was confused and he offered a shrug, although he also looked a bit embarrassed. I assumed it was because of my outfit. I wanted to keep it on, walk home that way, see what difference it made. Would men still look at me on the train? Would the conductor call me 'love' like he did every other time? Of course they wouldn't. But what if they weren't fooled like Drew had been? Would they turn a blind eye? Jay had told me that he never walked home in drag. He was at the back of the room and he waved, just as I was thinking about him. I grinned and waved back. The room was packed. I'd speak to him later. Another act was about to go on.

The room was quiet again but there was something wrong – some change in the atmosphere. Our table wasn't just quiet, it was *cold*. Drew looked mousey, sitting there in his uniform, his hair all over the place, hands in his lap, looking dead ahead at the stage. Lucy had her arms folded. Artie seemed to be on another planet, not looking at anyone in particular.

We sat through the next two acts and then there was some time to wait before the judges made up their minds.

I was going to get up and find Jay, just to get away from the tension, when Drew spoke.

'I'm sorry for missing your performance,' he said to me.

Lucy glared at him.

'It's fine!' I said. 'No worries.'

'That's why I'm in my uniform. I fell asleep and didn't wake up until hours later. I had to run to get the last bus.'

He was looking at me, but I sensed that his words were directed towards Lucy, so I looked at her and smiled.

'It's really fine,' I said. 'Lucy got a video, didn't you?'

'Yep,' she said shortly, and then, unable to hold it in any longer, she turned on Drew. 'I get it that you slept in,' she said, 'but if you were tired you could have set an alarm? I think you forgot about the slam. Or maybe you didn't want to come?'

Drew was shaking his head in denial. Artie turned round, suddenly interested in what was going on.

'No,' said Drew, 'I swear – I had wanted to be here. I just … it's been a really bad day … for lots of reasons, mostly my own, and –'

'What reasons?' said Artie, calmly, the slightest of smiles on his face. 'I'd love to hear.'

My God. Why were they being so mean to him? All he'd done was fall asleep! I started to tell them all again that it wasn't a big deal, but now they were ignoring me and looking at Drew, who was nervously touching the bridge of his nose, as if he was pushing up imaginary glasses.

'I … I got into trouble in Spanish class … there's been a lot of pressure lately … and …'

'Has there?' said Lucy. 'How come you haven't said anything to me about it? You've been avoiding me all day and now you stand me up and it's because of Spanish?'

'I wasn't avoiding you!' he pleaded.

I had to admit, it was a little odd that we hadn't seen Drew all day. He'd been in school but he didn't come and talk to us at break as usual, and he would hardly look at me in Spanish. Maybe Lucy was right. Maybe it was *him* that was acting weird.

'I'm not stupid,' said Lucy. 'Don't talk to me as if I'm stupid. I know where this is going.'

'What?' said Drew, looking genuinely surprised.

'You're going to dump me,' she said.

'Lucy!' I said, putting a hand on her arm.

'No, it's OK, Charlotte,' she said, shrugging me off. 'Your poem made me think. Men always treat women like this when they're about to dump them – making us think we're mental or whatever.'

She turned to Drew, who looked distraught. 'You're gaslighting me, Drew.'

She scraped back her chair, grabbed her bag and jumped up to leave, turning back to me for a second. 'Charlotte – you were amazing,' she said.

She turned to Drew. 'Goodbye. Do *not* follow me.'

'Wait!' said Drew, trying to grab her arm as she left. But she was gone.

Artie looked concerned. 'Charlotte – I'm going after her,' he said.

'No, Artie. I'll go,' said Drew.

'Fuck you, Drew,' said Artie, not even looking at Drew as he sped off.

It was just me and Drew at the table then. He looked crushed. I wasn't sure what to say. Had my poem really just caused them to break up? Why was Artie *so* mad?

Just then a loud voice silenced the room.

'Good humans of Buster's!' the man on stage began. 'I'd like to announce the winner of the very first Buster's Books and Coffee Poetry Slam Competition!'

All of a sudden the slam seemed silly, irrelevant even. I wished I wasn't sitting there dressed like a man. I wanted to be Charlotte again. There were a few words about the poets and the high standard, and then they announced the winner.

'And the winner is ... Sylvia Clements! Come on up here, Sylvia!'

Buster's went wild, clapping and shouting, and I rose to my feet as well to cheer for Syl. It was the right choice – her performance had been the best from the very beginning. I was glad not to have to get back on the stage. Drew was still sitting down.

'Come on, Drew!' I said, beckoning for him to get up and clap.

But instead he rested both elbows on the table and put his head in his hands. I sat back down again. I wasn't sure what to do. I could see his shoulders shaking slightly. *What would I do if it was Lucy?* I thought. I'd reach out – put my arm around her – ask if she wanted to talk. Maybe with Artie too. But it was different with Drew. I thought back to my poem – the man's voice accusing itself – the epitome of strength and power. I wondered what Drew had done, or what had happened to crush him like this. I couldn't just put my arm around him, and it made me angry for a second. It wasn't fair. But I couldn't just leave him sitting there and ignore him either, could I?

I gave him a little nudge. The kind of poke you might give a hibernating hamster to check if it's still alive.

He looked up, red eyed. 'Sorry,' he said. 'I'm fine.'

I nodded. He wasn't fine.

He stood up. 'I'm sorry, Charlotte. I'm getting out of here.'

He turned to leave and I wanted to tell him not to, but the truth was that I wished I could follow him.

He took a couple of steps and then turned and came back. 'How are you getting home?' he asked.

I shrugged. 'Train?' I said.

The station wasn't far from Buster's but it was late and the station would be almost deserted, and I was dressed in drag.

Drew must have been thinking the same thing. 'I'll wait outside for you. I just need some air, OK?'

'I'm coming with you,' I said.

I had just decided it. I wanted to leave too. I half expected him to say no, but he didn't, and we left together, past people beginning to stop clapping and taking their seats again for the closing of the evening, a presentation for the winner followed by a performance from the winner of a previous slam in Dublin.

As I left some people shot dirty looks at me, perhaps thinking that I was leaving because of sour grapes. Jay caught my eye from across the room and made a sad face. I assumed he was indicating that he was sorry I didn't win. I grinned and signalled that I'd call him tomorrow. He gave me a thumbs up and blew kisses.

Opening the door from Buster's was like being born. It wasn't that cold outside but the fresh air hit me right in the mouth and my skin tingled all over. Drew grinned out of the corner of his mouth, suddenly looking more upbeat. He must have seen my confused look.

He pointed to my face. 'Like the 'tache,' he said.

I smiled and smoothed down my whiskers. 'Thank you,' I said. 'It is a little itchy, though.'

'You didn't have to leave for my sake,' he said.

'I didn't. It was too noisy. And I'm absolutely wrecked. Train isn't for a while, though.'

We stood there awkwardly for a few seconds.

'Fancy a chip?' I said. 'My treat.'

'Hell, yes. I'm starvin'.'

'Shall we cut through the park?'

'Aye.'

Botanic Gardens was a lovely walk during the day, but I wouldn't have done it on my own at night. Still, as much as I felt safer with Drew beside me, I pulled off my moustache and wig and shoved them in my bag, shaking out my hair.

We walked in silence for a couple of minutes. I suppose neither of us knew what to say. We couldn't start a conversation about something else, given what had just happened, but I knew I didn't want to be the one to bring up Lucy. Finally, as we reached the gates of the park, Drew spoke.

'I'm sorry if I messed up your night,' he said.

'What? You didn't!' I said. 'But ...' I was going to ask him. I couldn't just leave it hanging. 'Is everything OK, Drew?'

It was dark in the gardens as we walked through but I thought I noticed him lowering his head slightly.

'No,' he said. 'It's not.'

I don't know if it was the darkness, or if it was just because I was still buzzing from having been on stage, but boldness was coming more easily, and so I asked him what he meant, and maybe he was feeling bolder too, because he slowed his walk and answered.

'I've messed everything up, Charlotte. Every single thing.'

'Wow,' I said. 'All in one day?'

I was trying to lighten the mood. It didn't work.

'No. It was something I did before today.'

'Before?'

'Yeah ...'

There was a pause. I heard him taking a deep breath. We were in the heart of the park now and there was a light at the other side – we could see it glowing in the distance – but there was no light where we were. We could see vague shadows moving on the path at the other side of the square of grass, but not much more.

'Fuck it,' he said. 'Charlotte, can we sit on this bench for a minute?'

So we did. I half wondered if he was going to kiss me. I suppose the thought came from out of the darkness, the way thoughts like that do. They sneak up on you at night. Stupid to think it. He spoke again and the thought moved aside.

'Did you ever have a secret that you really, really couldn't tell? Because it would just wreck everything? But having the secret also wrecks everything?'

I nodded. He could hardly see me, but I couldn't speak. The question was about him, not me, but I knew *exactly* how that felt.

'I did a thing and it's awful. So awful,' he said, putting his head in his hands again.

I knew that I was meant to be being a friend; I knew that I was meant to be listening to him. I should have been able to put my own situation to the side, just for a few minutes. But it was like the person I'd been on stage – the loud, brash man who needed everyone to hear his voice – it was like he had broken through. The voice that came out sounded like my voice, but I heard it as if I was someone sitting next to myself. There wasn't a moment – not even a second – between Drew saying 'I did a thing ... so awful' and the voice that came out of me. I didn't have time to catch it.

'Adam's bullying me,' I said.

I felt Drew's whole body turning around on the park bench beside me and his face was close enough to mine that I felt his breath as he exhaled.

'What?' he said.

I turned around too and remembered myself. 'I ... I shouldn't have said that. I'm sorry, Drew. You were saying something and I interrupted. I'm so sorry – it just came out, and it's nothing. What were you saying? You did something?'

'No! I mean, shit, Charlotte. Tell me about what Adam's doing?'

A plane passed overhead. I wondered where it was going. I wished I was on it. But where would I go? There were Adams all over the world. You would never know you'd met an Adam until it was too late and they were texting you videos of yourself, undeniable pictures of yourself, trusting them, saying yes. Could I trust Drew? I had no idea. I would never be able to tell if a man was trustworthy ever again.

'I'm not a good person,' he said, as if he'd read my mind. 'I've been so stupid. But listen, Charlotte, I'm being honest right now – *I'm on your side.*'

I looked at his blazer. The Stewards badge, dull in the darkness. He saw me glance at it and he took it off and put it in his pocket.

'I'm not a Steward right now,' he said. 'I'm your friend.'

I didn't know what he meant by that. You were either in or out of that group. And nobody ever left it. But even so, there was something in his tone of voice and the fact that he had been just about to tell me something really personal that made me want to believe him. And I suppose that's why I told him everything.

38. Drew

I couldn't stop her telling me. I didn't want to. I had entered the park with a head full of self-pity and a heart full of regret, and all of it had disappeared in an instant as soon as she mentioned Adam. Now we were in her world, thinking about her. Afterwards, when I thought about it, I'd feel shame that she was telling me, as if I was someone who deserved her confidence. But on that park bench, it was just us against the world and she needed me.

'I'm so sorry ...' I said, after she'd told me.

'It's not your fault,' she said.

I knew what she meant but I couldn't help thinking about this girl in my last school who'd sent her boyfriend a topless pic and then broken up with him. He sent it to everyone. He got into a shitload of trouble, but it didn't matter – everyone had seen the picture, including me, and when Jonny had shown me I'd laughed a bit and said 'Jesus, mate'. It could have meant 'It's so wrong of you to show me this', but it could also have meant 'Woah this is incredible' or some variation that the lads might've said if everyone had been there, looking. I had been deliberately ambiguous so that Jonny wouldn't know, so that I wouldn't embarrass him by saying that I didn't think it was right. And now, if he found out that I'd slept with his fiancée, it would make everything worse, because he wouldn't believe that I was sorry. Because I was that type, wasn't I? A *top shagger*, as Adam would say.

The truth is that, even though I knew it was wrong to send around a topless picture of someone like that, I hadn't actually *felt* it at the time; I hadn't felt sickened.

And now here I was listening to Charlotte, and when I told her I was sorry, I didn't just mean 'This shouldn't have happened to you', I also meant 'I hate myself for being the kind of prick who takes part in stuff like this'.

'You don't deserve this,' I said. 'It's awful.' I meant it.

'Thanks, Drew. Nothing I can do about it, though.'

I wanted to contradict her – to tell her to go to the cops, to tell the principal. But I didn't bother because I knew she'd have thought about that already, and who would want to risk a video like that getting out?

'Do you like him?' she asked me then. 'Adam, I mean.'

I fucking hate him, I thought. *If he was here now I'd tear his head off.*

'No,' I said. 'I can't stand him.'

'I understand why you're a Steward, though,' she said. 'And I get why everyone likes him. I just wish ...'

'That he'd step on a landmine?' I said.

She laughed. 'Yes! But only if I was watching. Or maybe he could just accidentally fall off the school roof or something?'

'Or step on a rusty nail, get gangrene and die really painfully?'

She was properly laughing now. 'Or maybe fall into the piranha tank at Exploris?'

'Yeah!'

We went on like that for a while, imagining increasingly horrible ways for Adam to die. It was funny at first but after a while we stopped laughing, and after another while we'd stopped talking altogether. I noticed how cold it was getting.

'We missed the train,' I said.

'I know,' she replied. 'I really wish I could kill him, you know.'

Her voice was steady, calm. It was a matter-of-fact statement. I wasn't sure how to respond.

'I mean, I wish I was the kind of person who would be able to do that,' she continued.

She was really thinking about it.

'But you're not,' I said.

'Nope. So he wins.'

We stopped talking again. I was trying to think about the train and how we were going to get home, but her last words had struck like a hammer. *He wins.* I wanted to tell her *There are always winners and always losers.* She'd said it as if she'd never had that thought before. I guessed that she'd always been a winner.

'Maybe not,' I said.

'Nope. Definitely.'

I turned to face her in the darkness. I tapped her shoulder, inviting her to turn towards me. 'Charlotte,' I said.

It was important that she heard this. *Really heard* it.

'If there are winners and losers, then he can be either,' I said, 'and so can you.'

'What's that supposed to mean?' she said.

I knew I wasn't making complete sense but I could see it now – she was on the losing team. But I knew if you were on the losing team that it was also possible to win sometimes. Everyone I knew knew that. It's why people bother applying for jobs. It's why Dale was doing his course. It's why my parents did the lottery and made me eat breakfast and filled in the application form to enter me for Cooke's. Sometimes it was luck, but sometimes it was just trying.

'It means that anything can happen.'

Her eyes widened. 'But there's no way out of this,' she said. 'There's no way we can win ...' There was a pause. She let out a short breath. And then she said, 'How?'

I was smiling and she couldn't see it, but I wanted to kiss her so badly right then, and not just because she was beautiful and smart and *here*, beside me in the park, but because I didn't know the answer, and I also did know it – the answer was *Screw him, we'll find a way.*

'I have no idea,' I said. 'But I am totally sure of two things. One: we need to find a way home, before the park gates shut; and two: we can't kill him, but karma's a bitch.'

She laughed. 'I like the sound of that, but I'm unconvinced.'

'Trust me. We'll figure it out.'

'Your optimism is incredible,' she said, but her tone was light.

She stood up. 'Come on,' she said. 'We'll walk to the bus station and get the Dublin Airport bus to Lisburn. We'll be home in an hour. And you can tell me *your* big secret on the way. One for one, right?'

'It's nothing,' I said. 'I don't think I want to talk about it after all, if that's OK? It doesn't seem important any more.'

PART TWO

March

39. Charlotte

It's amazing how you can just exist sometimes – just put your head down, drift through. Performing at the slam had bolted something on to my personality, something that made me able to keep going. I told Jay about it when he'd asked how Christmas had been. We had met at Buster's – he said to plan the New Year, but really it was just for coffee and gossip.

'It was fine,' I said.

'Just fine?' He raised his eyebrows.

'Yes. And that is totally fine by me.'

'I get it. No drama.'

'Exactly. This is going to be the Year of No Drama, Jay. Since the slam I feel really different. It's like, I just want to move on now – to grow up.'

'You sound determined.'

'I am. I have exams, I have coffee ...' I raised my cup to him. 'That's all I need.'

Jay raised his cup as well and we clinked them across the table. 'I will drink to that. You're strong, Charlotte. No drama!'

Of course, I didn't tell him that on my phone I had forty-two unread messages from Adam. Each one might be another threat. Ignoring them was taking half my energy, and the other half was concentrated on avoiding him in the sixth-form centre and keeping myself stable. Every time he sent me another message, every time someone mentioned his name, I tried to block him out. I thought of something else. Did something else. Studied. Played hockey. I learnt how to knit. I helped Mum with the housework.

The freezing winter gave way to a softer air. The cherry trees blossomed early. I began taking driving lessons. Artie's dad bought him a car and he picked me up most mornings. I thought about asking if we could call by Greenwood and pick up Drew, but I didn't. Since the night of the slam something had happened. Even though Lucy and Drew made up, Artie was still avoiding him. All he would say about it was that his boyfriend didn't like Drew. I assumed it must be jealousy and I didn't push it because our group had changed a little anyway. Artie had been seeing Crispy more often, and I had been lying low – preparing for my exams, keeping myself busy. I saw Drew sometimes, but always when he was with Lucy. I couldn't tell if that was deliberate on my part, or on his, but we hadn't spoken about what we'd shared on the night of the slam. I think both of us knew that there had been a closeness in the confession of that night that it might be dangerous to revisit.

A few days before our trip to Granada I was asleep in bed when my phone buzzed under my pillow and woke me up with the jolt that I now felt every time my phone made a noise. I stared at the bright screen, the words blurry at first. *Please don't let it be Adam.*

It was Lucy.

> Lottie! I heard something awful about Don Antonio from Richard. I don't know if it's true! You have to call me if you're still up!

I sat up, now wide awake. I could hear the TV downstairs playing Mum's drama series. She wouldn't hear me. I clicked on Lucy's name.

'Lucy? What's going on?' I said. 'Is Don Antonio OK?'

'Yes!' said Lucy. 'Or not. But I mean he's not dead or anything like that.'

'Oh. Good ... What's going on?'

'OK. Well ...'

I lay back on the pillow and listened. Lucy had heard it from Richard who had heard it from Adam who apparently had been drunk and let it slip that Don Antonio had paid for Drew's trip to Granada.

'But I thought the Stewards had chipped in for it?' I said.

'Me too, but Richard said definitely not.'

Richard was a Steward, one of Adam's best friends. They were often together, laughing in corners or making gross comments about girls behind their backs.

'But how would Adam know about Don Antonio if that was true?'

'Well, that's the thing,' said Lucy. 'It's Adam. He always finds this stuff out, doesn't he? He has dirt on absolutely everyone, apparently. Richard said he even makes Stewards tell him stuff so that he has ultimate power over them. I mean, who knows how he finds stuff out about teachers, but it sounds like it could be true, doesn't it? Don Antonio is always keeping Drew back for chats and things, and he practically *gave* him that iPad.'

I thought back to Adam's texts. *It's just a reminder of what we had.* I wanted to throw up.

'That makes it all sound so dodgy,' I said. 'Don A is just being kind. I mean, even if he did pay for the trip, is it really that bad?'

'What? Of course it is, Charlotte! It's uber-creepy and wrong! Why would he even do something like that?'

She was right. But still, I couldn't believe it. I thought back to that night at the park and what Drew had said. He had never brought it up again and I had never asked: *I did a thing and it's awful. So awful.* Oh God. It couldn't be this, though? It was too difficult to believe. Everyone liked Don Antonio. We'd known him for years.

'Look, Adam hates Don Antonio,' I said. 'We all know that. I'm sure this is just a misunderstanding – something Adam said as a stupid drunk joke maybe?'

He was cruel enough to make it up. I knew that.

'Maybe,' said Lucy. 'But what if it's true, Lottie? What if something's going on with them? It would explain why Drew and I still haven't … you know.'

'Lucy, just because you haven't done it together doesn't mean –'

'I know, but it sort of fits, right? I mean, if he's worried about everything … and it would explain why he's been such a crap boyfriend recently too?'

I didn't know what to tell her. Lucy had never been dumped in her life. I got why she couldn't just accept that maybe Drew had gone off her. But I knew something she didn't; I knew that Drew had a secret.

'Do you think we should go to Mr Baker about it?' I said.

It seemed mad. It was just a rumour. A rumour from an untrustworthy source. And if we went to the principal then he'd want to talk to Drew about it, obviously, and Don Antonio, and what if it was false?

But what if it wasn't false?

'I think we have to,' she said.

I knew she was right, but it was horrible.

'It's late, Lucy,' I said. 'I can't think about this now – my brain is mush. I'll talk to you in the morning, and we'll make a plan, OK?'

But I knew even then that I would find sleep difficult. My head was spinning with thoughts about Drew and Adam and Don Antonio, all saying things and hiding things, Lucy, needing to know the answers, my mum, needing to fulfil her plans for me. And somewhere in a dark corner of it all I was trying to remember myself, myself on the stage, being bold, my *self*, speaking out loud. On that stage I had felt like someone full of their own power. How do you hold on to yourself when all the other voices are shouting for your attention? I didn't just need to figure the problem with Adam out: I needed to figure *myself* out as well.

40. Drew

I couldn't wait to get to Spain. I'd never been away before –
not like that. We had to sort out a passport really quickly.
It cost a fortune but Mum said it was OK because it was a
huge opportunity. Dad wasn't massively comfortable with
the Stewards paying for the trip. He hated taking charity.
And a handout from a rich boys' club? That was hard for
him to stomach.

'This Stewards club must really rate you,' he said.

I knew he was putting a positive spin on it.

'Yeah,' I said. 'I reckon I have a good chance at that
scholarship.'

That cheered him up. I was putting the work in, doing
my duty. I was getting through it. I'd made up with Lucy,
just about. Maybe I was hoping that things really would
work out for us. I still liked her, and if I could just try a
little harder then maybe it would keep my feelings in the
right place. And I was trying to play the long game with
Adam. Every time I saw him I wanted to punch his lights
out, big time. But I kept my hands in my pockets, fists
tight, digging my fingernails into my palms. It became
harder and harder to play it cool, though. I hated him.

The main thing was keeping him away from Charlotte,
but Artie was always with her in school. Any time he caught
my eye he made sure to shoot me a look that said *Lay off*.
I was happy to oblige. I saw Dale the odd time around the
estate. He didn't give me any dirty looks. It was worse than

that. He just blanked me. It hurt. I missed him. Every time my phone went I hoped it was him. It was always Lucy.

Mum let me stay off school a couple of days before Spain. She insisted on taking me to town to get me new shorts and T-shirts.

'It's twenty per cent off today so we can't wait until the weekend – you'll just have to catch your work up. It'll be roasting in Spain,' she said. 'Your Aunt Irene gets the back burnt off her every time she goes. You'll need sun cream and a hat too.'

'I'm not seven, Mum. I'm not wearing a hat. And my old T-shirts are fine.'

But she couldn't be persuaded.

We had finished by lunchtime. I could have gone back into school for the last hour but I didn't want to. I'd spent all day walking around the shops behind Mum and thinking about Charlotte. Charlotte and Adam. Charlotte and me. She'd told me this awful, horrible thing, and I needed to make something happen to make her safe. But she'd told it to me. She had trusted me. It was awful, but also wonderful, and I knew it was wrong to feel it. I knew that there was nothing I could do to make a happy ending happen between us. The sooner I left school, the better.

'Do you want a wee cup of tea?' said Mum before I'd even gotten through the door. It was always the first thing in our house. A wee cup of tea. Whatever had happened, whatever was about to happen. And it didn't matter if you said yes or no, you were getting one anyway.

I slumped on the sofa and checked my phone. Nothing. I scrolled down the old messages. It had been months since I last spoke to Dale. The last messages from him were about the engagement party. Karen would be almost ready to have her baby by now. How can a baby, a whole person, happen so quickly?

Mum came in with the tea and a plate of biscuits. 'I'm going to take mine upstairs,' she said. She liked to be alone with her women's magazines sometimes.

I continued scrolling through old messages. Adam, Dale, Charlotte, Lucy ... I couldn't just *decide* to dump Lucy, any more than I could *decide* to leave the Stewards. Any more than I had *decided* to join them in the first place or to go to this stupid school.

'Thanks, Mum,' I called as she headed up the stairs.

'Ok, love. I'll iron those new clothes for your suitcase later.'

Why do people iron clothes before they fold them up and put them in a small box on wheels? Why do people iron clothes at all? Mum even ironed pillowcases and pants.

I sipped the scalding tea, took my notebook out of my bag and started writing, in Spanish, a list of what I'd do if I had the choice – things I could do if I was really free.

> Go to university without going to Cooke's first.
> Ask Charlotte out.
> Write poetry in English. Become a writer.
> Tell people I am a poet.
> Travel around the world until I found a place where I could start over again.

I took another sip of tea. My phone buzzed. It was a text from Lucy.

> Hi Drew. You weren't in today. Hope every-
> thing is OK. Coming out later? ILY.

Woah. ILY? She hadn't said it before. Neither of us had. *I love you.* I had only ever said it to one girl. I swallowed more tea, letting it scald my throat. Why did everything only ever get more complicated? I couldn't say it back. Not when I had just been dreaming about dumping her. I took my tea up to my room. Mum had left the small suit-case on the floor. It was lying open and empty except for my brand-new passport. If only I could grab it now and just fly away to anywhere else. Instead it lay there, open-mouthed, accusing me, mocking me for being excited about a trip which was only going to mess things up even more. I'd promised Lucy that we'd sleep together in Spain. And it's not that I didn't want to, exactly. But I'd messed everything up enough already. It would make things worse. She was expecting it, though. Adam was expecting it. He'd paid for my trip. Who was I most afraid of? And the answer wasn't allowed to be 'myself' even though it should have been.

41. Charlotte

We had decided to tell Mr Baker. Both of us knew it was the right thing, but sitting through Spanish in the morning was the absolute worst. I couldn't look Don Antonio in the eye. Either he was completely innocent and we were about to torpedo his career, or he was a creepy perv who was grooming a student. That hour seemed to last for ever.

As it happened, when Lucy and I went to Mr Baker's office at break time, he wasn't there.

'He won't be back until next Wednesday,' said his secretary without stopping her typing.

'But we'll be in Spain then!' said Lucy, a hint of distress in her voice.

The secretary, Mrs Jackson, looked up and stared at Lucy over the top of her glasses. Her lips were pursed. She was not in the mood. 'Well, you'll have to wait until after your trip to speak to him. Would you like to make an appointment?'

'No, it's OK,' said Lucy with an exaggerated frown, clearly not taking the hint that Mrs Jackson couldn't care less.

Mrs Jackson went back to her typing without saying anything else and we stood there for a few seconds before realising that the discussion was over.

'What are we going to do?' whispered Lucy on the way back to the cafeteria.

I shrugged. 'I don't know. I suppose we'll do it when we get back from Spain?'

'But Drew and Don Antonio are both going on the trip!'

Sometimes Lucy speaks to me as if I can solve impossible problems. How was I meant to know what we should do? I tried not to sound annoyed. I knew she was just worried about Drew.

'I don't know, Lucy. I suppose it will be OK as long as we stick with Drew and make sure he's not alone with Don Antonio. Who knows, maybe we can use the trip to see what we can find out? It might be better to wait for a bit to tell Mr Baker. It's still just a rumour.'

She smiled sincerely. 'Thanks, Charlotte. I think you're right. You're always right.'

'I'm not,' I said, but I was too tired to try to convince her.

Had I been right to tell my secret about Adam to Drew, and not to her? It didn't feel right. She was my best friend. But there was something about Drew that seemed more adult than Lucy – like he wasn't going to freak out about it. Thinking about him this way just made me feel worse, like I was betraying Lucy, even though I hadn't done anything wrong. I tried to shake the thought off, even though I knew it would return before long.

42. Drew

There were orange trees everywhere. They lined both sides of the main street that led to our hostel. The girls were complaining to Miss Robinson because we'd had to walk so far from the bus stop and it was raining a little and all of them had tons of luggage. She looked a bit stressed out herself, but all I could think about was the orange trees just growing there with fruit that looked like it was about to drop, and I wondered what happened when it did drop. Did people just help themselves? Annoyed commuters were walking in suits with their AirPods in, trying to weave in and out of our shambling little group. The girls had given up on Miss Robinson.

'Sir! Can we stop for a rest, please? SIR?'

'No, no, it's close now. Let's keep on,' said Don Antonio.

'Sir, I'm *freezing*!' said one of the younger students.

'Slight exaggeration, Clara, but you're dressed for the Costa del Sol!' he said, waving his hand dismissively. 'I warned you. It's Spain, but it's not time for bikinis. It's raining!'

'I know it's raining, sir!'

A group of Spanish teenagers in jeans and sweaters giggled as we walked past. Most of the girls in our group had sun hats, sunglasses, crop tops, high heels. They were lumbering along dragging huge cases.

I put out my hand to the girl who said she was freezing. 'Here – I'll take your case.'

She looked surprised but handed it over immediately.

'Well done, Drew,' said Miss Robinson. 'Very gallant!'

Lucy beamed at me.

'Bloody hell, what's in here? Did you bring a pile of Spanish dictionaries or something?'

The girl screwed up her face. 'It's just a bit of make-up.'

'I love all these orange trees!' said Charlotte.

'Me too,' I said.

Younger students rolled their eyes in exhaustion as Don Antonio directed us across the road and pedestrians tutted at our slow struggle to get moving. Don Antonio ignored them. He was in a great mood. I couldn't remember the last time he seemed so happy. He led us to the hostel and gave out room keys.

'Sorry, Drew,' he said, giving me a keycard. 'It was uneven numbers so you're on your own. You can swap with someone else if you like but let me know first, OK?'

I saw Charlotte and Lucy exchange a look that I didn't quite understand. Maybe it was sympathy. I didn't mind being on my own, though. I could write without anyone seeing and there wasn't anyone I'd want to hang out with. Well, maybe one. I looked at the girls taking selfies together on the sofa in the reception area and tried not to wish that Lucy wasn't here.

'¡Bueno! OK, guys!' Don Antonio clapped his hands to get our attention. 'So tonight we go to see the play *Yerma*, and before this we have dinner ... let's see ...' He looked at his phone. 'You have three hours to explore your rooms and the local area. Go out in pairs, please, and take your info packs. There's a map inside and the school mobile number. Back here at 5 p.m.?'

There was a flurry of activity and the reception area was cleared in seconds. I shouldered my bag and moved towards the staircase to find my room.

'Drew!' It was Lucy, catching up with me on the stairs. 'Charlotte and I are going to head out to find some shops. You coming?'

'OK, I'll just leave my bag down.'

'I can't believe you got a room to yourself!'

She grinned widely and this time I knew exactly what the look meant.

'Yeah, amazing,' I said.

I was going to have to figure out a way to avoid having time on my hands. Suddenly my small bag felt three times heavier. This was meant to be a time to sort things out – to finally get my head cleared. I could never get away from myself, though. The ability to screw things up seemed to follow me around.

The rain had cleared by the time the girls had finished doing their hair and make-up. It was warmer now and they began debating whether or not to return to the hostel to change.

'Oh, don't roll your eyes, Drew! Maybe it's about to get super-hot, and I bought sun clothes especially,' said Lucy.

'Let's just keep on,' said Charlotte. 'Maybe we can get new stuff in the shops!'

Lucy did a little squeal and they grabbed one another's arms and went ahead of me down the narrow cobbled side street.

But the shops weren't open.

'It's the middle of the day!' wailed Lucy.

'Siesta. I forgot,' I said. 'They won't be open again for an hour or so.'

The girls looked majorly disappointed.

'Come on, like,' I said. 'Look at this place – it's insane.'

We were standing in a small square, the sun glancing off every passing car, blinding us. Thin passageways disappeared from the edge of the centre where we stood – steep, uneven paths that wound into darkness around tall buildings made of old stone. The façade of a church with a giant clock, people sitting under trees, old men reading newspapers and young people eating fat slices of pizza cross-legged on the wooden benches. Buildings became rock, leaning against the skyline. Small buses and cars shooting up the hill, too fast, into the dark tunnels of side streets.

'Let's walk up a hill and see what's up there,' I said.

The girls agreed, although they didn't like the look of how steep the streets were and how narrow the footpaths. It was either that or go back to the hostel, though. So we walked – at first, chatting about the days ahead, about when the shops might be open again, about the play we were going to see, and then soon becoming quiet, concentrating on the walk as we started getting out of breath. Everything kept on going up. At home you could see where you were going – a hill has a brow, and you knew that when you reached it, it would start to level out. The narrowness of the streets here meant that we only had a few metres of vision. Each turn only took us higher, past the back yards of tiny flats with more orange trees, the odd bar with rusty chairs under a white-umbrellaed table. It was a labyrinth and we were following an invisible line from the start to an end that we couldn't visualise.

'I need to stop,' said Charlotte. 'You two are machines!'

'I'm not,' said Lucy. 'I'm knackered too. This is wild!'

It was a good place to stop: a stone bench at the side of the road. I unscrewed the cap off the water I'd brought and offered the girls a drink.

'Lifesaver!' gasped Lucy, taking a long drink and passing the bottle to Charlotte. 'Best boyfriend ever!'

We sat in silence again for a minute and then there was music. At first I thought it must be coming from a nearby bar, but then it sounded higher up – above us somewhere. I saw Charlotte looking up too.

'Let's go and find it!' said Lucy, jumping up and pulling her hair back with a scrunchie.

'You recovered quickly,' I said, as she pulled me and Charlotte to our feet.

'Just a bit dehydrated, that's all!'

Around the corner a path veered from the road, and the path became steps. There was a handrail which we clung to. The steps were so steep that we leant forward to stop ourselves from falling back. And then we were on a small cobbled square, with stone benches on the grass verge and a couple of thin trees. A handful of young people sat in a group on the grass making daisy chains. A boy in a blue shirt and a baseball cap sat on a bench, legs crossed, playing the guitar.

Charlotte had crossed the square and was looking over railings. 'Oh my God, guys. You have to see this!'

Above the corrugated tile rooftops, a bright-green skirt of forest held up a giant palace. Great big slabs of cool cream and terracotta spread against the clear sky, looking down on us even though we were exhausted from climbing so far up. The Alhambra palace, like a crown on top of the city. I felt the thrill of being so very far from home. The boy playing the guitar began to play something faster, more rhythmic. Some of the girls started shouting in appreciation. One began to clap. At first it seemed like she was out of time with the tune, but then she stood up and walked over to the boy with the guitar and he was stamping his foot and her clapping started to sound more like a conversation with the song. Another girl stood.

'¡A bailar! Sonia!' she shouted.

She took over clapping as the girl began to dance in the middle of the square. The boy with the guitar smiled, eyes closed, and he played louder as she stamped and twisted and the dust rose in soft clouds beneath her feet. Charlotte and Lucy were still looking at the Alhambra, but I could not take my eyes off the dancing girl, or whatever it was that was happening to her. It felt like there was nothing at all between the turning of her fingers, her arms, her hips and the music – as if she could stop moving and the tune would automatically stop as well. She'd been smiling when she started but she now had a look of intense concentration, the way a young child looks when she's trying to say something new for the first time. And the voice of what was happening was saying something to me in a language I didn't understand but never wanted to stop hearing.

'What do you think, Drew?' Lucy elbowed me sharply in the ribs.

'Ow! Eh?'

'I said, we should ask Don Antonio if we're going to visit the castle. We should, shouldn't we?'

'Um, yeah.'

The dance had finished. Sonia had bowed to the musician, who nodded to her and clapped in appreciation. I wanted to clap as well, but I was frozen.

'Hey, stop looking at that sexy Spanish babe!' said Lucy.

Her tone was light but I knew she kind of meant it, and I couldn't explain that I hadn't been looking at the dancer like that. I mean, it wasn't that she wasn't attractive, it wasn't even that she was attractive *plus* talented ... It was something else – beyond everything –

something that made me come away from myself, almost like I was with her in the music, even though to everyone else I just looked like another guy watching her from the sidelines. I couldn't explain it to Lucy at all, so I grinned and kissed her cheek and said, 'Don't be silly,' and she put her arm around me and everything went back to everyday normal, even though we were miles away from our everyday lives.

Later, at dinner in the common area of the hostel, Don Antonio sat beside me. Giant pizzas filled the centre of each of the small round tables so that there wasn't any room for plates. We ate off paper napkins and put our cans of lemonade on the floor. Lucy and Charlotte had come in late and had to sit with a couple of first-years. Don Antonio and I were with two students from my Spanish class.

'So,' Don Antonio began, 'how was everyone's afternoon?'

'Boring,' said Jane. 'The shops were shut? We just went back to the room and watched Netflix.'

The other girl nodded, mouth full of pizza.

Don Antonio shook his head. 'You're in one of the most beautiful cities in Europe, and you watched Netflix?'

'*Friends*, season nine.'

'Man,' he said, faking utter depression. 'Not even a new show?'

They giggled.

'What about you, Drew? Please tell me you found something more interesting than Netflix?'

'We walked up the hill,' I said. 'Like, for ages. And we saw the Alhambra.'

He nodded, picking up an enormous slice of pizza with both hands. 'And what did you think of that? Isn't she incredible?'

'Yes,' I said. 'Amazing. And there was a dancer.'

'Oh? Flamenco?'

'I think so. There was this guy busking and he was brilliant, but then she just got up and started dancing. Like, it wasn't planned or anything, she was there with her mates, and she just ... started.'

I sounded like an idiot. Talking about some girl instead of the incredible palace and the view over Granada. The other two students exchanged a look and stifled giggles. But Don Antonio was chewing his pizza and still nodding away, like I'd said something profound.

'I know, I know,' he said, gulping his Coke. 'It's magic, right? It's a magical place. Wait. I'm going to get you something you need to read. Be right back.'

He jumped up from his seat and left. The other two kids gave me a 'What was *that*?' look and I shrugged. Don Antonio was really excited to be here. I guessed that he was just feeling good because it was sunny and he was in his home country. He returned a couple of minutes later with a bunch of paper and sat down at the table again.

'Here,' he said, straightening the sheets of paper on his knee and handing them to me. 'Duende!'

'What's that?'

'Duende? It's the word Lorca used to describe the magic you experienced in that girl's dance. Just read it, OK? Not now – later, when you have a minute. It will explain the magic.'

'It's ... in Spanish.'

'Yes, of course. I can help you. It's better in Spanish.'

I thanked him and looked at the papers. I didn't particularly want more Spanish homework, but it gave me a bit of a buzz to know that he thought I'd be interested and could manage it. As I turned to put the script in my bag I saw Lucy and Charlotte staring at me from the other side of the room.

43. Charlotte

'Oh my *God*, Charlotte, there is clearly *something* going on!'

I thought it looked odd too, to be honest. Don Antonio and Drew sitting together. And they were talking so intently, heads close. Then Don Antonio had sprung up and returned with some papers for Drew. What would it have looked like if we hadn't already suspected something going on, though? Would we have even noticed it?

'OK, look, it could still be innocent,' I said. 'Maybe he was just returning homework?'

'On a school trip?'

I shrugged. 'I saw Miss Robinson marking papers on the bus?'

But I knew that Lucy had a point. We had both noticed that Don Antonio had given Drew a room on his own. And Drew had been so quiet all day. *Some*thing was up. He hadn't even been that interested in that view of the Alhambra, and that was the best thing we'd seen all day. My phone buzzed. Probably Mum, I thought, checking that we'd all got there safely. But the text wasn't from Mum.

How's sunny Spain? Miss you already.

Oh God. I had forgotten. I had momentarily let myself imagine a world without him. He had attached a photo. A still from the video. A waterfall of pain crashed over me. I burst into tears.

'Oh my goodness, Lottie! Are you OK? What's wrong?' Lucy put her arm around me and I saw some other kids looking over. I needed to get out of there.

'Follow me!' I hissed between big gulps of air, trying to calm myself down. I took Lucy's hand and led her out of the room. I had no idea what I was going to say to her, but it didn't even seem important. I just needed to get out of that place, away from people, as if I could get away from anything, as if I could ever get away from him. I sat down underneath the big tree in the open courtyard in the middle of the hostel, head in my hands. Lucy sat beside me. I wasn't ready to tell her yet. I wished that Drew was with me instead because at least then I wouldn't have to explain it again. I knew I'd done nothing wrong, but I did feel ashamed. That picture. What if my mum ever saw it? What if Drew did? Or Lucy?

'So, what's wrong, pet?' said Lucy gently.

I lifted my head. 'It's Adam,' I said.

'*Adam?*'

'Yes. He's been ... pestering me to go out with him again.'

'Oh, love!' She gave me a big hug.

I suddenly felt so tired. I leant into her shoulder and felt that if I closed my eyes I would fall asleep right there under the huge tree and never wake up.

'It's OK,' I said. 'I mean, it's not, but it will be. I'm OK really.'

'Boys are so stupid,' she said, stroking my hair. 'I mean, *of course* he regrets dumping you. Who wouldn't!'

'He didn't dump me,' I said, too tired to explain any-thing else.

'Of course not,' said Lucy in the kind of tone a mother might use to console a sad toddler. 'He's an idiot. And he'll get over it, I'm sure.'

'I know.'

People had started to file out of the room where they'd been eating. We got up. I thought that we'd gotten away without making a scene – nobody was really looking at us. But my phone buzzed again and this time it was Drew.

You OK?

I could see him at the back of the line of students. I caught his eye and quickly texted back:

Yes. Speak later.

Don Antonio's loud voice sounded over the chatter before we could see him. 'OK, everyone! Pay attention for a moment!'

The group went quiet.

'So I hope you all enjoyed your pizza!' A cheer went up and he settled everyone down with a wave again. 'Good, good. We'll be leaving for the theatre in thirty minutes. Go and get yourselves ready. You don't need anything, but if you're bringing a phone and it goes off in the theatre you'll be joining Señor Lorca in the world beyond, yes?'

There was laughter.

'That's it! Thirty minutes! Don't make me come looking for you!'

'Thirty minutes?' moaned Lucy. 'That's just about time to do make-up. What about clothes?'

'You'll have to go naked,' said Drew, joining us with a smirk.

'Oh, you'd love that!' I told him.

He half laughed and Lucy went red. But even though he was grinning I thought I saw something in his eyes momentarily, some kind of glance towards me, that said the opposite of his smile.

'Let's go then!' I said, blinking it out of my mind. 'We can't go to the theatre in rags, can we?'

44. Drew

The theatre was right beside the Alhambra. It was in the basement of an enormous hotel. I'd never been to anywhere so posh. Even Henry Cooke Academy looked like a total dump in comparison. There were marble pillars all over the place and there was this elaborate design on the stone walls – red and brown interlocking lines that went on and on over them. Don Antonio said it was done in the Moorish style. I'd have been happy just to look around the hotel, imagining the kind of people who stayed in places like this, and wondering how much it cost to stay here for the night, and what the rooms were like.

'It's exquisite, isn't it?' Don Antonio said. 'Some day when you're a famous writer you'll come and stay here.'

He winked at me and I saw Lucy and Charlotte exchange a look. The same kind of look as before.

The man from the hotel reception led us down steps and we gathered at the theatre door. He told us about the history of the place – how Lorca would visit the hotel theatre to see his friend Manuel de Falla, a composer who used the piano in the theatre.

'You are standing where he stood,' he said. 'But *Yerma* is not a play about wealthy people who came to places like this. Who knows something about this play?'

A couple of first-year hands went up. 'It's about a woman who can't have a baby, sir.'

'That's right,' said the hotel man. 'And it's about more than this.'

More hands went up. 'It's about a woman and she kills her husband, sir.'

'True!' he said.

'Spoilers!' shouted one of the older students.

'You were meant to read it before we came, Niall!' said Miss Robinson.

Everyone laughed.

'Charlotte,' Don Antonio said, 'tell us a bit more – what's this play really about?'

Charlotte's cheeks went pink but she didn't hesitate to answer. 'It's about patriarchy. It's about what society expects of women and how if you don't conform you might as well be dead. Or kill someone.'

Everyone laughed when she said that, including Don Antonio, but I noticed that she wasn't smiling, and my thoughts went back to dinner. It was Adam who'd upset her earlier. I knew it.

'¡Muy bien!' said Don Antonio. 'Well done, Charlotte – absolutely correct. Let's go in, everyone, and remember what I said about your phones!'

It wasn't long before the curtain rose in the dark room. On the stage a woman lay asleep in a dreamy half-light. There was deathly silence, and I wanted to laugh out loud. I felt like a child, almost having to put my hand to my mouth to stop me from giggling. When they started to speak, it was so serious, and the words were about marriage and having babies. I wanted to leave – it was all so quiet. I thought about Karen. I felt sick and I tried to concentrate on the play. Five minutes in and the characters were already talking about breastfeeding and death and infertility. I wanted to laugh and puke. I could feel the back of my neck getting hot. I thought about home. So far away. And then something else happened.

On stage the two women who were talking about having babies were joined by a teenage girl, and as they spoke the girl said that she wasn't interested in having kids because she wanted to be free, and one of the other women asked her why she'd got married then, and she replied, 'Because they made me. They make everyone.' And when she said it, I got this picture in my head of Karen and Johnny getting married – Karen in a white dress, massively pregnant, the two of them at the altar and all our friends in the church, watching. It was only a few weeks away. Nobody was forcing them, but I remembered what Karen had said about her and Jonny getting married: *We just thought it was the right thing, you know?* And I thought about how I understood it, even though we all knew that it was OK not to get married these days and that people didn't even care that much if a teenager had a baby. What made her feel like it was the right thing? What made me understand it?

I could breathe easily from that point in the play. It felt like I needed to watch it then, to see if it had the answer. The language became deeper; it was like being inside a poem – I couldn't understand all of it – and the characters got bigger and madder until the end, the inevitable death. And no answers – only more questions. I was shaking when the curtain closed and everyone stood up, and I stood up too and we all clapped, and Lucy nudged me out of my trance and whispered, 'Are you OK?' and I realised that my face was wet.

I wiped it with my sleeve. 'Sorry, yes, I'm fine.'

She laughed. 'No need to be sorry,' she said. 'Look. Charlotte cried too.' She nodded towards Charlotte, a few seats over from us, and I saw that she was wiping her face as well.

45. Charlotte

The walk back to the hostel was quiet. Well, it was quiet for us. The younger students were laughing and chatting to Miss Robinson as if they'd just been to the cinema to watch the latest romcom. They were discussing which of the actors they fancied most and how weird the play was with all the singing and people running around in a forest wearing masks.

'Philistines,' said Don Antonio to Miss Robinson with a half-smile.

'But, sir, that wee woman with the mad hair!' said one of the second years. 'Did she look familiar to you, sir?'

'Yerma. Her name is Yerma. You know, the title of the play ...'

'Aye, yer ma!'

The kids exploded with laughter.

'Yes, yes, it's very funny ...' He was pretending to be dismissive, but you could see he was enjoying the craic. But Drew, Lucy and I didn't have much to say. I wondered if they were thinking about the play like I was. Lucy had tried making conversation, but it didn't go anywhere and she'd given up.

When we got back to the hostel she took me aside. 'I'm going to see if Drew and I can slink off now, to his room, you know?'

'Oh wow,' I said. 'Is this what I think it is?'

She squeezed my arm excitedly. 'I hope so!'

It looked to me like Drew's mind was a million miles away. He was sitting at a table near the tree tapping his phone.

'OK, love,' I said, squeezing her back. 'Good luck.'

'Thanks!' she said, kissing me on the cheek before lightly skipping across to where Drew was sitting.

He smiled to see her approach but something in it looked uncertain. A couple of minutes later she had walked off on her own, head down, towards the rooms. Drew looked at me and then looked away. I followed Lucy and found her sitting on her bed. As soon as she saw me she burst into tears.

'He doesn't want me, Lottie! What's wrong with me?'

'What? Nothing!' I said, throwing an arm around her. 'What did he say?'

'Some stupid thing about that play having really affected him. For God's sake. Couldn't he have just said he had a headache like a normal person?'

'Awk. Come on.' I held her tightly. 'The play was full-on. He'll come round in a bit. I'm sure of it.'

She looked up, all hopeful. 'You think so?'

'Of course. He's sensitive. That's why you like him, isn't it?'

She sniffed. 'I suppose so.'

I handed her a hankie, hoping that I was right and that it really was just the play. I could believe it, though, because after that performance Timothée Chalamet could've walked into the hostel and I'm sure I would have ignored him.

'Here. Come downstairs again, let's get a Coke?'

Lucy shook her head. 'Thanks, Lottie, but I just want to go to bed, OK?'

She did look shattered.

'OK. Do you want me to stay with you?'

'No! You go back down. You can keep an eye on Drew and Don Antonio.' She started to cry again. 'Oh God, Lottie, do you think that's why he doesn't want to be with me? Do you think it's because of him?'

'No. I honestly, really don't think that. But I will keep an eye on them both, OK? I promise.'

I sat on her bed for a few minutes more, wondering if I should stay or go, but she insisted that I leave. I decided I'd go for a while, not long. She was right about keeping an eye on Drew.

The two of them were now sitting near the tree. Everyone else had gone to their rooms – it was just Drew and Don Antonio. They seemed happy enough to see me, though.

'Join us!' said Don Antonio before I had even asked if I could.

He pulled out one of the chairs and I sat down. It was getting dark and the moon was just about visible in the small square of sky above the courtyard where we sat.

'The play,' said Don Antonio. 'What did you think, Charlotte?' He was sipping a tiny cup of coffee.

'Ah ... um ... it was good ...' I said. He'd put me on the spot. I glanced at the table and saw that there were papers spread over it, and I wondered if they were the ones he had given Drew earlier. 'I mean, really good,' I said. 'It felt ... I don't know, weirdly relevant.'

'How?'

Now he was asking. What could I tell him? I looked at Drew and I knew he understood.

'It's how things are,' Drew said.

I breathed deeply. He was trying to help me out. Don Antonio looked at him.

'I mean, it's no different these days, really. We still expect girls, women, to behave in certain ways, to do certain things.'

'And men?' said Don Antonio.

'Yeah, men too. But it's, like, worse for women.'

'How?'

Neither of us answered.

'OK, so the play was relevant,' said Don Antonio. 'But so is everything. We can read a newspaper and it's relevant. What *moved* you, Charlotte?'

God. He wasn't going to let this lie. The moon above our little square of courtyard was brighter now. The oranges looked ripe and heavy. I was suddenly so tired. I thought about the character, Yerma, in anguish, strangling her husband, and I felt heavy as well, and then something in me dropped, like the orange, and I said, 'I felt like she did, sir. I wanted to kill him as well.'

Don Antonio raised his eyebrows but I wasn't finished.

'I knew how she felt. Like men own everything. They control everything. Even when they don't want to, even when it's bad for them too, and that isn't fair, but it's even more unfair on women.'

'Yes,' he whispered. 'Yes.'

We were quiet again for a minute and then it was Drew who spoke. He was looking at me when he said it. 'I don't know if I should say this. I don't know if it's OK to say it, but it's what Cooke's is like.'

Instead of looking shocked, Don Antonio nodded in agreement and it was me who said, 'What do you mean?' even though I kind of knew.

Don Antonio nodded again to let Drew know that it really was OK to speak.

'Well. Just that … I mean, I'm not saying that boys treat girls any better where I come from …' He wasn't looking at either of us but at the table. 'But at Cooke's it's so … extra controlling. Like, the Stewards, you know?'

'What about them?' said Don Antonio.

I shot Drew a look. He couldn't tell about Adam. Please, no. Not like this.

'I mean they go around blackmailing people. Did you know that, sir?'

'No, I didn't,' he said, raising an eyebrow. He took a sip of his coffee. 'Do you want to tell me what they've done, Drew? If you do, I have to pass it on – it's not a choice.'

No, Drew, I thought. *Don't. Give* me *the choice. Don't take it away from me.*

Drew looked at me and shook his head. 'I can't give details – it wouldn't be right,' he said. 'But they have stuff on everyone. On me too.'

They had? What stuff? The stuff Drew hadn't told me about yet? What could he have done that was so bad?

'They paid for my trip, sir. Did you know that?'

Don Antonio nodded. 'I did. But I didn't realise they were intimidating you.'

I took a breath, relieved. A bright-green bird flew out from the tree and broke the peace of the night and all of us jumped slightly.

'Don Antonio,' I said, 'the Stewards are telling people that it was you who paid for Drew's trip.'

Drew's mouth widened. 'They *what*?'

'I'm sorry, Drew. I should have asked you about it but I only heard the other day.'

'That's not true!' Drew said. 'Why would they say that?'

Both of us looked at Don Antonio, who calmly took another drink of his coffee. He crossed his legs, set the cup down on the table and folded his hands together. 'Drew, Charlotte,' he began, 'I did not pay for Drew's trip.'

'I know!' said Drew, still boiling.

Don Antonio frowned. 'I am going to guess that it was Adam who started this rumour?'

I nodded, mouth closed. He sighed and looked up at the sky, and then back to me. 'He is, let's say, not my greatest fan.'

Drew's eyes widened. He was staring at Don Antonio.

'Are you OK?' I asked him.

He glanced at me. He looked like someone who'd just been slapped. 'This is it! This is how he's getting revenge!' he said.

I looked at Don Antonio. His forehead was wrinkled up. 'Revenge?' he repeated.

'Look at this!' said Drew.

He pulled his phone out of his pocket and spent a minute scrolling. Then he held the phone towards us. It was a text from Adam:

> … he'll get what's coming in the end. You know he tried to get me suspended one time for telling a joke about him being a pedo? … Total snowflake.

Don Antonio took a deep breath.

'That little *shit*,' said Drew. 'He used me to get at you.'

Don Antonio nodded slightly.

I didn't say anything. I couldn't. We had tried to go to the principal about it, but the worst thing was that if we

220

had reported it to someone else this would all have been over. I felt the guilt rise up like acid in my throat. It would have been easy to prove that Don Antonio didn't pay for the trip. We had kept quiet. We had allowed Adam to keep the rumour going.

'Are you OK, Charlotte?' Don Antonio asked me.

I shook my head.

Drew seemed desperate. Bewildered. His hands were tightly balled fists. 'I can't even do anything about it!' he said. 'I can't do anything.'

'Hey,' said Don Antonio, turning to Drew. He put a hand on his shoulder – a gesture that would have confirmed all my suspicions about an hour earlier. 'It's OK,' he said.

'It's not!' said Drew, distraught, tears now flowing down his face.

'It will be. I promise,' said Don Antonio.

'We have to stop him. He's *evil*,' said Drew.

'We will sort it out, Drew.' Don Antonio was speaking softly, trying to calm him down, and it made me think back to the first time Adam sent me the video – how trapped I felt, how much I wanted to scream and vomit every time he texted me. There was something in Don Antonio's voice – something strong and confident – that kept me from crying as well.

'He seems invincible,' he said, 'but he only has the power we give him. It's all anyone has.'

I didn't know if I believed him. Yerma had to kill her husband because she didn't have any power – they had taken it all.

'Don Antonio,' I said. 'I know it's getting late now, but would it be OK if I took Drew for a walk? Just down to the square and back? I think it would do us both good.'

He looked at his watch. 'OK, then – but just to the square. Don't tell the others, OK? I'm only letting you two go because you're seniors and I trust you. Back in forty-five minutes or I'm calling out the search party, yes?'

46. Drew

I knew I couldn't stay at Cooke's a moment longer. It was over. I had to get away from that place and those hateful, awful people. Fuck university. I could get a job. I wasn't stupid. I could work hard. It would be OK.

Charlotte didn't say anything as we walked down to the square and I was glad, because my head was spinning. I wondered what she was thinking.

We reached the square and I had expected it to be quiet. It was late now, dark, but the air was warm and the breeze was like close human breath, comforting but not cool. There were people sitting around the square on benches and on the ground. Some older men chatting and smoking pipes. But it was mostly young people, laughing, talking, sharing food, kissing. We found a free bench beside a group who were gathered around a man who was juggling with what looked like wooden clubs which were on fire. The group seemed to know him and they were shouting his name and cheering. The fire spun in the air and lit up the faces of the juggler and his audience.

'You OK?' Charlotte asked me.

'Yeah,' I lied. 'You?'

'Not really,' she said.

She drew her knees up under her chin and I wanted to put my arm around her so badly that I sat on my hands in case I forgot myself again.

'I think you should tell Don Antonio about what Adam's doing to you,' I said.

'I know,' she said. 'But once I tell him, the video will get passed around. If Adam gets caught, he'll do it. They won't be able to stop him.'

I couldn't argue with her. I knew she was right. One way or another he was intent on hurting her.

'I wish we could take that fire and burn him,' she said. 'I wish we could just make it stop. Even for a while.'

'You need a night out with the lads,' I said.

'What?' She laughed.

'Bottle of Bucky in the park. That's what we do. Don't you have anything like that?'

'Like, drinking?'

'I don't know. Anything.'

She rested her chin on her knees and stared at the juggler, who was finishing up and taking a bow then dousing his fiery sticks in a bucket of water.

'No,' she said. 'I had the poetry slam. But it's hard to write at the minute. I can't.'

'I write poems too, you know.'

She sat up and let her legs drop to the ground. 'You serious? You never said!'

I shook my head. 'They're for my eyes only.'

'No way! You dark horse. You'll show me, right?'

'No way.' I laughed.

I didn't add *because some of them are about you.*

'Come on, Drew. If I can get on stage in man-drag and read my poems then you can show me yours.'

I looked at her face. The moonlight, silver on the stone square, outlined her shape.

'You're so much braver than I am,' I said.

I held her gaze for a moment and then I made myself look away, past her, to the girl who was talking to the juggler, and Charlotte turned around to see what I was looking at.

'Didn't we see her earlier?' she said, a little too loudly. The girl looked over at us.

I turned away but it was too late: she'd seen us and knew we were talking about her. She smiled widely and walked over.

'Hi,' I said, looking up at her. 'Sorry – we weren't really talking about you.'

She laughed. 'Yes, you were!'

It was the dancer from the square. She had very black hair and, like the others, she was dressed in bright patchwork-type clothes, the kind you see people wearing at festivals. She had a dark-pink scarf tied around her head, trailing at the back. I was too embarrassed to speak, so it was a relief when Charlotte stuck out her hand and the girl shook it.

'I'm Charlotte, and this is Drew.'

'Hi!' she said, offering her hand to me too and doing a little curtsey. 'I'm Sonia.'

'We saw you dancing earlier – up there.' Charlotte pointed to the steep hill behind us.

'Ah!' Sonia said, nodding vigorously.

'You were amazing!' I added. It came out all at once and made me sound like an enthusiastic six-year-old.

Charlotte and Sonia both smiled.

'Thank you,' said Sonia. 'Where are you from?'

I said, 'Belfast' at the same time as Charlotte said, 'Northern Ireland.'

'We're on a school trip,' said Charlotte.

'You're here to find Lorca?'

'Yes.'

'Well, that is interesting,' said Sonia.

She turned to her friends and shouted, 'Hey! Miguel! Elly! These guys are looking for Federico!'

Her friends gave a round of applause but it didn't seem sarcastic. I tried to imagine any of my friends feeling that proud of someone from Northern Ireland. Or even reacting to a stranger like that, without laughing at them. It made me feel small and unsure of myself.

'Well, you're in luck,' Sonia continued. 'Here!'

Suddenly she grabbed my arm and took out a Sharpie from her pocket and wrote something on me: @soniacueva2004.

'Instagram,' she said, clicking the top back onto the Sharpie. 'Party tomorrow night – just next to that square where you saw me dancing.'

'Ah, we really can't,' said Charlotte. 'Thanks, but ...'

Sonia shrugged. 'OK, but you know, if you want to find your Lorca – he's there. Right, Miguel?'

The juggler, a tall boy with brown skin and very dark eyes, wandered over and slipped his arm around Sonia's waist. 'Sí. The poet is said to haunt the cave. You really should come.'

'I don't think we can,' said Charlotte. 'If our teacher found out we were messing around in a spooky dark cave ...'

'It's not spooky!' said Sonia. 'It's my uncle's house!'

Charlotte laughed.

'It's true. People live in the caves up there – you should see them. I mean, even during the day, if you can't come to the party – come and visit, right?'

Charlotte said thank you and that we might, but I knew that she had no intention of going. We said goodbye to Sonia and Miguel, and as soon as we were out of earshot

I said, 'I'm going. You don't have to, but I'm definitely going.'

'Come on,' said Charlotte, slowing as we trudged up the cobbles towards the hostel. 'Think about Don Antonio. What if something happened to us? He'd get into tons of trouble and it would be our fault.'

She was right. But I was sick of Cooke's – sick of the endless rules and having to do what was expected. It wasn't Don Antonio's fault, but it wasn't mine either, and I had literally nothing to lose. Soon enough the people who still liked me would stop liking me when they found out what I'd done, and then what would I have? I could at least take this one moment – this one opportunity to live a bit – to find something in a place that I would probably never return to.

'Well, we'll just have to make sure that nothing happens to us then. Nothing bad anyway.'

I linked arms with her to lighten the mood and I could feel the hairs on her forearms tickle against my skin.

She laughed. 'I'm definitely not going with you,' she said. 'As far as I'm concerned, we didn't even meet those circus people tonight.'

It was my turn to laugh. 'Circus people?' I said.

'You know what I mean,' she said. 'I don't know what you'd call them. Alternatives or something. With their fire-eating and whatever.'

'Juggling!' I said.

'Aye. And they live in caves. Like, we're a long way from Cherry Valley, aren't we?'

'OK, boomer,' I said.

By the time we reached the hostel we were laughing so hard that we had to wait five minutes before we went inside to calm ourselves down.

47. Charlotte

I had no intention at all of ending up at that cave party. Exploring the Alhambra palace with Lucy the next day, we wandered around staring at the intricate mosaics and marble patterns, the sun blazing. We moved slowly and sat down frequently to stop ourselves becoming dizzy with the heat. The last thing I felt like doing was going to a party, even if it hadn't been a really bad idea to begin with. So, hours later, when Drew and I found ourselves climbing that steep hill again as the sun was fading, he could have been more understanding.

'Stop worrying!' he said. 'It'll be fine. Don Antonio's gone to bed, Lucy's asleep, nobody will even know we've been out. We'll just stay for an hour. I just want to see it.'

I wanted to see it too. We had walked past some cave houses earlier in the day. A man who didn't speak much English came out and tried to get us to give him a couple of euros to go inside and look. Lucy didn't want to – she was frightened by his forwardness and I practically had to run to catch up with her again. She had spent the whole day moping and worrying about Drew.

'Talk to him!' I'd said at lunch. 'He's your boyfriend, Lucy. If you think something's wrong you've got a right to ask him.'

I didn't mean it to sound sharp, but we were in this incredible place, and maybe it was selfish, but I just wanted to enjoy it as much as I could.

'It's probably hard for you to understand,' she huffed. 'Boys always treat you like a queen.'

If only she knew. But I held back from telling her. It wasn't the right time. I hadn't even told her that I'd slept with Adam, and I should have. Drew knowing and her not knowing – it was wrong. I wished she wasn't causing me to think about it.

'Sorry,' she muttered. 'That was unfair.'

She half-smiled and I returned the gesture to let her know it was OK.

'Do talk to him,' I said. 'There's something I need to tell you about, though. C'mere.'

I put an arm around her to draw her close. She leant in and I told her about Adam and Don Antonio.

'Oh my actual *God*! That is awful.'

A couple of kids looked over.

'Sssh,' I said, whispering, 'we can't tell anyone, OK?'

'Of course not! I mean, wow, though. I can't believe Adam would do that, can you?'

I shook my head, unable to verbalise the lie. 'Hey,' I said, 'at least it means that Drew's not in trouble, though?'

'Yeah,' she said glumly. 'I mean, obviously I'm glad, but it also means that he's definitely gone off me. He doesn't have any other reason to not want to hang out with me. He didn't even sit with me at breakfast.'

'We were late to breakfast!'

'Would it have killed him to save a seat?'

And it went on like that for the rest of the day. It was a relief to leave the hostel with Drew in the evening. We'd invited Lucy but she thought we were mad to sneak out. So it was just us, heading back up the narrow, darkening streets, towards the top of the hill.

'I'm exhausted. Can we stop here for a sec?'

Drew turned and came back to where I was sitting on a roadside bench.

'Sorry,' I said. 'The Alhambra really took it out of me today. And then Lucy ...'

Drew frowned.

'What's up with you two?' I said.

It was taking a chance, I knew. I didn't really have the right to ask him. But it was his turn to tell me something personal on a bench in the night-time. And I'd let him persuade me to go to this daft party. He definitely owed me something.

He sighed and looked at his feet. 'Everything's a bit of a mess at the minute, Charlotte. And, I mean, Lucy is *great*, she really is, but I'm finding it a bit hard to ...'

'To cope with the pressure?'

He looked up at me. 'Yeah. And also ... I'm just not really sure what I want right now. You know?'

I did know. And I wanted to ask him what his big secret was, but the conversation felt so serious, and even though it was cooler now, we still had quite a climb ahead.

'Come on,' I said, springing up. 'Let's go – I don't want to be out too late.'

'You've changed your tune!'

'I have. We both need some craic, and like you said, nobody needs to know about it. Do you think that cave houses have doors?'

'What? Of course they do, you eejit.'

I wasn't sure whether it was fear or excitement, this fizz in my stomach. I was breaking the rules. But maybe this was me now. Maybe if I could get on stage, dressed like a man, speaking my truth as a woman, maybe I could do anything really, and it was only fear that had stopped me in the past. Maybe I'd get into trouble, but that was probably going to happen anyway, and when Mum and the school found out about the video my life would be over. Whatever happened at the party, it might change everything or nothing, but it wasn't going to make things worse, was it?

48. Drew

Sonia was out front when we got to the cave house. She gave us both a big hug and I could smell alcohol on her breath. I looked at Charlotte but she didn't seem bothered. I wondered if she'd ever been drunk. It reminded me that this was the first party I'd been to since Karen and Jonny's engagement. Here we were now – high up above Granada, on a warm cliff top, the night approaching, loud music, loud people and the flicker of lights inside. It seemed a million miles away from Greenwood estate and Cooke's, and I couldn't have been happier about that.

Sonia led us inside to get drinks. It wasn't what I had imagined. Much more like a house than a cave, but not like a modern house – more like one of the cottages at the folk park at home: low ceilings, thick whitewashed walls, old-fashioned wooden furniture. Chairs lined the wall in a large room that didn't seem to have any other furniture except some tables stacked up at one end.

'My father runs a restaurant here,' Sonia said, handing me a tin of beer. 'They have flamenco for the tourists.'

'Do you dance here?' I had to shout over the music.

She shrugged. 'Sometimes. If I want some money? But mostly it's dancers from out of town.'

I bet they're not as good as you, I thought.

'Anyway, enjoy! Have fun!' She hugged us both and left to join her friends.

Charlotte and I clinked beer tins and the music changed.

'Oh I love this song! Come on, Drew, dance with me!'

It was a side to Charlotte I hadn't seen. I followed her into the space where others were dancing and, without even thinking about how I looked or who was watching, we were jumping around to a pop song. It was more fun than I'd had in a really long time. *If Dale could see me now*, I thought, but no, I wouldn't think about him, or about anyone. I just wanted to hold on to this moment – be right in it and not think about anything or anyone else. So we danced like mad and when we were knackered we grabbed another beer and sat down.

'Hey, look!' said Charlotte pointing at the wall opposite us. It was a framed picture of Lorca. 'It's the ghost!' She laughed. 'Hold my beer, I'm going to find the loo.'

So I sat there with the two cans, one in each hand, looking at Lorca and everyone dancing. My brain was pulsing with the music. I finished off my can and crushed it. It was a combination of the music and the beer, the colours all around me, people dancing, the red and orange lights flickering off white stone walls – it was hard to keep my eyes open. Despite the noise, I wondered if I might lie down on the row of chairs for a bit. Charlotte, on the other hand, seemed more alive than ever. She came back from the toilet with another girl and another drink – a glass of red liquid with a slice of lemon floating in it.

'This is Carla, Sonia's cousin. She's going to show me the roof garden. You coming?'

'It's very nice,' said Carla. 'Great view.'

I shook my head. 'I'm just going to stay here. We should probably get going soon, Charlotte.'

Charlotte did a big fake frown. 'It's OK – I'll be a good girl!'

Carla giggled. 'Hey, Drew,' she said as she led Charlotte off. 'You ever been in a cave house before?'

I shook my head.

'Well, explore the place – it's cool – have a look around.'

They left and I still had Charlotte's half-drunk beer in my hand so I sipped it. It was so warm and my head was spinning. As I moved from room to room the beer in the tin disappeared without me noticing.

The big room for dancing led out to a narrow corridor with lots of doors on either side. I went into the first room, half expecting to see people getting together, but there was nobody there. There was an old iron bed and a huge wooden wardrobe and not much else. The big door creaked as I left the room. Someone squeezed past me in the corridor.

'Oh, perdóname!' said a girl.

She shot me a suspicious look as the big door clomped shut behind me. I thought about explaining that Carla had told me I could explore, but she was gone before I could remember the Spanish words. I decided I'd only go into one other room. It was a bit weird creeping around in a stranger's house, but I wanted to see more. The door at the end of the corridor was set back slightly from the wall. There was an awkward step down before you could reach the handle to open it and I crept inside.

The door shut heavily behind me and in the flicker of a lit candle on the dresser I could see the outlines of a bed, a table. There was a smell – sweet and heavy, like the white flowers at a funeral – and I scanned the room to see where it was coming from. I could hear the distant noise of laughter, the pulsing bass of the pop music. I turned to leave the room, to return to the party, and there on the wall before me was a huge face. Flickering in the candlelight, it made me jump and then I laughed at my own fright. It was only another picture of Lorca. Huge, though, each eye the size of a football.

I felt so tired, and the scent of the lilies was filling my head and making me want to lie down on the bed. Maybe I would sit down, just for a minute? It couldn't hurt. Just for a minute.

The bed was too soft. I sank deep down as I sat, and I knew if I lay down I would fall asleep. There was something written underneath the picture in Spanish. I thought if I tried to translate it it would keep me awake. I couldn't understand the whole thing.

> No man ever fell backwards to death. But ... I
> have seen ... unpublished life ... plans, like the
> buckets of an endless waterwheel.

It was the word 'endless' that got me, I think. I read it again. Everything around me and inside me melted away to leave only this moment, the two of us facing one another in the dark. There was no party, no noise, not even any thoughts of anything outside that door. I could almost hear my own heart beating.

Unpublished life. Like my poems. Like all the stuff I should have done and didn't. It was a kind of death, obsessing over it all. It was stopping me from going on – all this waiting for people to find out, letting people like Adam control me. I was suddenly terrified of all the things I'd wasted – all the times I could have just said no or been honest. When was I going to stop dying?

There was a banging on the door and then a voice, pulling me suddenly back to the real world. 'Hey? Drew?'

It was Charlotte.

I rushed to the door and opened it. 'I need to talk to you,' I said.

'Oh God,' she said, her face dropping. 'Are you OK? You look terrible.'

I rubbed my face with my hands. 'I'm OK,' I said.

And I was OK. That was as much as I knew.

'Can you smell that?' I said.

'What?' She looked confused and I understood why, but everything was clear to me now. Everything made sense, and I didn't feel afraid of it.

'I want to kiss you,' I said. 'Is that OK?'

And she didn't answer but she nodded, and before I could kiss her she took my face in her hands and pressed her mouth to mine.

49. Charlotte

His mouth was cold and it shocked me into sense. This wasn't right, no matter how natural it felt. I broke off the kiss and apologised, but I hardly meant it. It was impossible, but just for a moment, it felt really good to do an impossible thing.

'Don't apologise,' he said. 'I shouldn't have asked. Come on, let's go.'

He was grinning so widely but I'd never seen anyone look so white. I wondered if he'd been smoking drugs or something after I left him. I hoped not. What would I do, stuck up a mountain with someone who was high as a kite? I checked his pupils but I couldn't remember if they were meant to be big or small when someone was on drugs.

'Is everything OK, Drew?' I asked. 'Something seems a bit, I don't know, *off*.'

'I'm OK,' he said. 'I'm actually feeling *great*!'

It wasn't the most reassuring thing he could have said, but at least he could walk, and he did seem pretty much OK, apart from the weird spaced-out look.

'What were you doing in that room?'

'I don't know. Just having a look? Carla said it was OK. I just sat down for a minute. And then ... Anyway, it doesn't matter. Let's leave. We need to talk.'

He was keen to go right there and then. I thanked Sonia and she hugged me and we promised to keep in touch on Instagram.

'You kissed me,' said Drew as we set off down the hill.

It was past midnight. The air was cooler now and I was glad of the slight breeze.

'Look,' I said, 'it can't happen again, OK? It really just *can't*.'

'I know,' he said.

'Then why do you sound so happy?'

'Because you kissed me.'

'You're weird.'

He took my hand and I didn't pull it away. We were in a different country. There was nobody around who we knew. What could it hurt to hold hands for a few minutes? I wasn't thinking of Lucy. I wasn't thinking at all.

'You like me,' he said. I could hear the smile in his voice.

'I do,' I said, squeezing his hand. 'But this can't happen.'

'It is happening.'

'Well, then, once we get to the square it's over, OK?'

'Deal,' he said. 'And that's when I'll tell you what I've got to tell you. And then you won't like me any more. But for now let's pretend that there is nobody else. Just us, on this hill.'

It didn't feel like much to just put everything out of my head for a minute. I tried not to think about what he meant about me not liking him any more.

Walking slowly, partly because the road was so steep, and maybe also to make it last, we pretended that there was nobody else and nothing else, and for a few minutes on the quiet hillside I felt perfectly happy and free. Any time I had a thought or a memory, any time I started wondering what his big secret could be, I focused on my hand in his and I let the thought go. I detached from every-thing real, but this was real as well, even though it would disappear at the end of the night, like Cinderella's ballgown and coach, and after that we would only think of it as a fairy tale that had finished without a proper ending.

50. Drew

We floated down the hill, her hand in mine, the heat of it warmer than this afternoon's sun roasting the marble palace, the floral scent from the cave room still in my head. The sight of the square made my legs feel suddenly heavy. I knew that Charlotte was right. There were all sorts of reasons why we couldn't continue. But even though I was sticking to the ground now, there was still space in my chest to breathe – a feeling that I hadn't known had been missing. Whatever had happened in that dark stone bedroom had put it there – this ability to inhale and exhale freely. I was about to blow everything up. And it was going to be terrible. But everything was going to be all right.

'Hey, is that Don Antonio?' Charlotte dropped my hand. 'Shit, is it?'

It was. He was sitting in the square – the only person there. He was looking up at the full moon, low and yellow in the sky.

'We can't get past him!' There was a slight panic in her voice.

'It's OK. He won't stay out here all night. We'll wait in the shadows until he goes.'

We picked a dark spot on a bench underneath a tree. I wanted to pick up her hand again but I knew that now it was time for me to tell her the truth. I just said it, just like this: 'Charlotte. I cheated on Lucy.'

She frowned. 'I know. But it's over now. We won't do it again,' she said.

'I don't mean tonight. I mean, I slept with someone else.'

Charlotte's mouth opened as if she was going to say something but nothing came out, and I had more to say, so I kept on talking.

'It was the night of my ex's engagement party, months ago. It was ... an accident, but –'

'You don't accidentally sleep with someone, Drew!'

I saw Don Antonio turn around and Charlotte lowered her voice again. 'How could you do that? I mean ... it was wrong what we did, but at least it was only a kiss ...'

'I know, I know,' I said, hands held up. 'I was drunk, and it was so totally wrong, but I did it anyway, and I'm so sorry about it. I really, really regret it.'

'Oh my God,' said Charlotte. 'So that's why you've been weird about sleeping with Lucy? Do you love this other girl? I mean, did you even use protection?'

I took a deep breath. 'No. She was already pregnant.'

'What the fuck, Drew? Is it yours?' She was trying hard to whisper.

'No! No it's not. And I've spoken to her and we both really regretted it. It's such a huge mess, Charlotte. The girl was my ex and her boyfriend is my friend. *Was* my friend. He won't be when he finds out.'

'You absolute *dick*!'

I'd never seen her so angry. But I had expected it. And there was something else I needed to tell her. 'Look, I need to tell you another thing and I'm telling you because I don't want you to be angry with him. He only didn't tell you or Lucy because he wanted to protect you, but ... Artie knew about it.'

'Artie knew?' She was in shock. 'How?'

'His boyfriend was in the band that night.'

Her mouth fell open as the information clicked into place. 'I can't deal with this, Drew!' she said.

She stood up to leave, but she couldn't walk across the square because Don Antonio was still there, still sitting looking at the moon, like one of those human statues that you throw money at to make them move. Charlotte walked off the other way.

I went after her. 'Come on, Charlotte. Don't run off. Wait. Please.'

She turned around. 'I'm so angry, Drew!' She burst into tears.

My instinct was to hold her, but I knew I didn't have the right. 'I'm really sorry.'

She had her hands over her face and when she looked up her eyes were gleaming and narrowed. 'I can't believe that Artie knew and didn't tell me. I can't believe that.'

'Please. Please don't blame him. He was really struggling with whether or not to say anything. He knew it would hurt Lucy. And he knew I regretted it. All that pain would have been for nothing.'

'But it wouldn't have been for nothing, would it?' she said.

And I understood her, then. What we'd done together – the kiss. It wasn't a mistake for me, at least it didn't feel like a mistake. I meant to do it. But it was different for Charlotte. I'd made her a part of a betrayal that was wider than just me and her sharing a kiss, and she hadn't even known it.

All I could do was repeat 'I'm sorry'.

We sat down on our bench again. Charlotte had stopped crying but she still had her head in her hands.

'How am I going to tell her?' she said.

'I'll do it,' I said. 'I owe her that much at least.'

'Are you going to tell her about what happened between us tonight?'

'No. But I will if you want me to.'

'I don't!' she snapped.

'Well, then we can just forget it happened,' I said.

There was a silence for a few minutes, and I wondered if Charlotte was thinking the same as me, that I would never forget this night for as long as I lived.

'Why did you tell me?' she said finally.

I thought back to the dark bedroom in the cave. To the words I'd read, as clear as the moon. 'Because I've done everything wrong, Charlotte. I had a good opportunity at Cooke's. A chance to make things work. And I messed it all up. I just want to start again now. Even if it means everyone hates me. I'm going to leave school and I'm going to start again.'

'You're leaving school? I sincerely hope that doesn't happen, Drew.' The voice made us both spin around. It was Don Antonio. We'd been so lost in ourselves that we hadn't heard him coming over.

'Oh,' I said, standing up and brushing down my shirt for some reason. Trying to look respectable, I suppose.

'I didn't see you there. Look, I know we're not meant to be out and this is all my fault, OK? I begged Charlotte to come with me and –'

'Relax,' he said, waving me to sit down again.

He sat down beside us.

'Sir, I am *so sorry*,' Charlotte said. 'But as you can see we were on our way back.'

'Really,' he said, looking at her, 'it's OK. We can go together. In a minute.'

He seemed older, somehow. There was a sadness in his voice.

'Are you OK, sir?' I asked.

He flinched in surprise. 'Me? Heh.' It wasn't really a proper laugh. 'To tell you the truth, Drew, I'm thinking of leaving school myself.'

'No!' Both of us looked at Charlotte, who shrank a little. 'I mean, sir, don't leave because of Adam. We'll back you up – we know what he's like.'

Don Antonio shrugged lightly. 'There are things I need to do, things I should have done already.'

'*Like the buckets of an endless waterwheel*,' I said, mostly to myself.

'You know that poem?' He looked surprised.

'I read it ... it was just a quote on a wall,' I said. 'Well, I tried to read it. I didn't get very far.'

Antonio smiled and tipped his head to the moon. 'It's called "In the Garden of the Lunar Grapefruits". I've been thinking about it all evening. You should stay at school, Drew. You can weather it out. Think of it as a training ground. It's different at university – you will have more freedom. You could go on to further studies.'

It was my turn to shrug. Surely there was nothing left to say. Everything was screwed up and I just had to face what was coming.

51 .Charlotte

I sat on the bench drifting from being angry with him to hating myself, but as the pendulum swung from one side to the other, enough time passed for me to think that maybe he was right, maybe it was time to start over. I just felt so tired. Not just because of the long walk and the party. When Don Antonio said he was going to leave it was like him announcing the Adam Bailey victory parade. On and on it would go. Who would be next? But I had something that nobody else had. I had a way to make it stop.

'What if there was a way to get rid of Adam. Would you stay then?'

Don Antonio was silent. Drew took my hand again and I pulled it away. I was still angry.

As I spoke the words I had never felt more broken and more powerful. 'Don Antonio, I have proof that Adam's been bullying people.'

'Oh?'

'There's a video. He ...' I balled my fists and closed my eyes. Fuck him. 'He filmed us having sex. I didn't know he was doing it at the time. He's using it to bully me now.'

I opened my eyes and looked at them both. Drew nodded. He tried to take my hand again, and this time I let him.

Don Antonio blinked slowly and exhaled. 'Charlotte,' he said quietly, 'this is a very serious thing. You know that I can't keep it to myself?'

'Yes,' I said. 'I've got all his messages. It's evidence.'

'It's not just bullying,' said Don Antonio, rubbing his eyes. 'It's against the law.'

'I know,' I said.

'How long has this been going on?' he asked.

'Since the start of the year. The school year, I mean.'

He shook his head. 'I'm so sorry,' he said.

That's when I started to cry. It felt incredible. To finally just know that it was going to be over. I knew that once Adam found out he'd send the video out of spite. But I had been so afraid of that little part of me that he owned, and suddenly, as I spoke it out loud to Don Antonio, I felt all the other pieces of my life return to me in some way. He no longer had it all.

52. Drew

I didn't sleep that night. I kept going over what had happened. The party, the cave bedroom, then me telling Charlotte, Charlotte telling Don Antonio. The entire evening felt like I'd dreamt it, but I was wide awake. I fretted over how to tell Lucy. I tried to write it down, but it was too awful. By the time it was light I was ready. I wasn't afraid – I just wanted to get it done. I had imagined myself approaching her after breakfast, maybe taking her to my room, and just laying it all out.

But in the end I never got to do that.

Charlotte and Lucy were always late for breakfast. And lunch. And dinner. But this morning it looked like everyone was going to be late. When I stepped out of my room into the long hostel corridor a crowd of kids from Cooke's were outside their room. As I got closer I discovered the reason. Lucy was yelling. Really yelling. I wasn't even sure it was her at first, but in between shouting she was sobbing, and then Charlotte would say a few words and she'd start yelling again. I could make out words like 'secret' and 'boyfriend'. First- and second-year students were giggling and shushing each other, trying to get a better listen. I spoke to them firmly – told them to clear off – and they immediately turned to leave.

I was on my own, outside the hostel room where Lucy and Charlotte were having the row of the century.

'I just can't believe that you would do that!' shouted Lucy. 'You're such a liar!'

'I'm sorry. I'm so sorry.' Charlotte was crying. 'You're my best friend and –'

'Oh, we are NOT best friends.'

Oh no, I thought. She should have let *me* tell her about Karen.

'I'm really sorry. I was thinking of waking you up last night to tell you and maybe I should have, but –'

'You're only sorry because I've found out!'

'I'm not. Drew was going to tell you this morning himself. '

'Oh, how nice. Talking about me behind my back. God this is so *humiliating*!'

'Artie only knew that I knew because I messaged him last night. I didn't know until then. He shouldn't have told you. It wasn't his place.'

'Artie? What the hell are you talking about?'

There was a silence. And then Charlotte spoke again. 'I'm assuming you got a message from Artie?'

'Who else knows? Does the whole school know?'

'God, no. No! I swear. This is a mess ... Look, Artie only knew because his boyfriend was doing a gig that night and he saw Drew go off with Karen. I didn't even know until last night myself. None of us wanted you to get hurt, Lucy, please believe me.'

'What?'

The word was spoken so quietly I almost didn't hear it. There was another silence. I didn't like this.

'Who the *fuck* is Karen?'

'I ... isn't that what we're talking about?'

'Who's Karen?'

I wanted it to stop. I wanted to burst in and just tell Lucy that it was me, all me, that I was the person to yell at, not Charlotte, but I was stuck to the spot. At the far end of the corridor a cleaner was slowly moving from room to room with her giant trolley, oblivious to the bomb that was about to go off in Room 56.

'Who is Karen?'

'She ... she's his ex. You have to talk to him about it ... Lucy. Lucy, look at me, please. If we're not talking about Karen then –'

'You know,' she said.

I knew as well.

'This.'

There was a pause. I couldn't figure out what was happening.

'I ... I ...'

'You what, Charlotte? You didn't know anyone was taking your picture? You couldn't wait to kiss my boyfriend? Or was that a big mistake too, like not telling me about this *Karen*?'

I could hear Charlotte crying quietly.

'Never. Speak. To. Me. Again.'

The door opened suddenly and a wild-eyed Lucy stood staring at me. 'And the same goes for you, you disgusting creep.'

On the word 'creep' her voice broke and she ran off in the direction of the stairs, and I had never felt worse about hurting anyone in my entire life. I stood there looking into the room at Charlotte, sitting on the bed, hands covering her face, shaking, and I wondered what the right thing to do was. Which girl should I go to? Whatever I decided to do, it was going to be the right thing, and the wrong thing as well.

'Charlotte,' I said.

She looked up from the bed, and her crying got louder. I went into the room and closed the door behind me.

53. Charlotte

It was a photograph on social media. Sonia had tagged me with the message 'Keep in touch, guapa'. She wasn't to know that Drew wasn't my boyfriend. I had no idea that anyone had seen us. Everything was ruined. I sat there sobbing, Drew with his arms around me. It wasn't just sadness or guilt, it was rage. Anger. Because I'd been so stupid. To think I could casually give in to how I felt for just one night. To think that it wouldn't hurt anyone.

It was time to leave Granada for home. The rest of the day was a matter of keeping my distance from everyone. Don Antonio kept on shooting me concerned looks, no doubt worried that I was freaking out about our conversation the previous night. But telling the principal about Adam was a future crisis, and this was a current one. Drew and Lucy also kept away from me and each other. Both buried themselves in their phones. I wondered who they were messaging. Were they talking about me? How much worse could this all get?

I kept out of the room while Lucy packed and then I went in to get my own stuff. I stuffed it into the suitcase, remembering how carefully I had packed it last weekend, how excited we had been. Lucy had left the make-up she had borrowed from me on my bed along with a T-shirt that I'd given her as a birthday present a few months earlier. It was lime green with pink piping on the sleeves and neckline. She wore it all the time. I imagined myself unpacking the case and seeing it again, and I decided to leave it in the room.

At the airport I tried to read the book I'd bought but the words kept floating away and I soon gave up and put it into my bag.

As our flight was called, I moved closer to our group. Some of them were rifling through bags trying to find their documents. One or two noticed me approaching. Their faces looked serious and I saw one of them nudge a friend who looked up. As I got closer more and more students began to stare. Half of them had heard Lucy and me arguing. They'd all know about it by now.

Miss Robinson waved to me. 'Charlotte. Good. You're the last one. Come on, we've got to get on the plane.'

I glanced at Drew, expecting a nod or some small gesture of the solidarity we now shared as mutual assholes. But instead he widened his eyes and jerked his head as if to tell me to join him. This was risky. Or maybe he felt we had nothing to lose. I hoped he knew what he was doing.

'We need to talk. Now,' he whispered.

The kid in front of us half turned, as though she'd heard and was trying to hear more.

'I don't think that's a good idea,' I whispered back.

I started to take out my phone and he put his hand on mine.

'What are you *doing*?' I hissed.

'Sssh,' he said. 'Don't look at it.' He glanced around and then looked at me again. 'Hang back.'

'What?'

'*Hang back.*'

He grabbed my arm and we let the group walk away from us towards the gate, much to the annoyance of the eavesdropping third-year student.

'What's this about?' I said, knowing that we only had a brief moment.

'Give me your phone,' said Drew.

'What? No! Why?'

'Trust me,' he said. 'Give it to me. Please.'

His *please* sounded desperate. I handed it over and he put it in his pocket. He looked to see how far away our group was, and then he took my hand.

'I'm really sorry about this, Charlotte. It's awful. But I need to tell you now, before we get home.'

'What? Just tell me!'

I had guessed it already, though. Lucy had shared that picture of Drew and me kissing. She'd let everyone know what horrible people we were. I knew it when everyone started to stare.

But I had guessed wrong.

Drew took a deep breath. 'Adam's sent the video. It's online.'

54. Drew

I will remember her face as it was at that moment for ever. Destroyed.

I didn't know what to say. The airport was loud and people were knocking into us as they hurried to the gate. Neither of us moved. She started to shake. I put my hand on her arm and she lifted her eyes to mine, full of pleading and panic. I pulled her towards me, mostly because I couldn't stand to see her so helpless. Out of the corner of my eye, I saw Miss Robinson stressed out, helping a young kid empty their bag, presumably looking for a passport.

'We have to go,' I said into her hair after a few seconds.

We broke off and she picked up her bag, trying to steady herself. We turned to walk off.

'Wait.' She put down her bag and I turned around again. 'Did you see it, Drew?'

'What? No! I mean … No, I wouldn't have ever …'

I hoped so hard that she would believe me. Because it did come up in my timeline. I saw the thumbnail. And it made me want to be sick.

55. Charlotte

I walked when I could not walk.
I walked past their twisted faces:
Disgusted
Appalled
Revolted
Leering
I walked onto the plane
Like filth on someone's shoe
Spread out along the aisle.
They were going to be sick.
I was going to be sick.

I told myself, just a couple of hours in this metal container. That is all. I can do it. I can sit down and close my eyes, and concentrate on breathing, and try not to think about what they'd seen. Try not to think that it was for ever and that I could not erase it. Breathe. Breathe. Breathe. Not so much a mantra as a prayer. How could I continue?

A hand on my shoulder.

'Charlotte.' It was Don Antonio. 'Lucy asked me to swap seats with her. Is it OK if I sit beside you?'

I couldn't even nod my head, couldn't even look at him. Did he know too?

He squeezed into the seat awkwardly. 'I can see you're not OK,' he whispered. 'I'm assuming it's what we spoke about last night?'

Suddenly he seemed like the only person I knew who I could trust.

'The video,' I whispered. 'It's out.'

As soon as I said it out loud I burst into tears. As I cried it felt like the terror of everyone knowing, everyone seeing, entered my body and it wasn't me making this noise, it was the fear, howling like a banshee. I was aware that the plane was quiet, or maybe it was the white noise at the edge of where my sound stopped and the rest of the world began. All I could hear was the roar of that silence and, beyond this, something groaning deeply, and I didn't want it to stop because as long as it kept going it was all that I was and it was easy and natural.

Eventually the static died down and I noticed my breathing: steady, deep. I felt a hand on my back and a voice that said, 'Not much longer. We're almost home now.'

I wished that *home* meant the end, or some kind of escape at least, but my eyes burned when I opened them. Everything looked exactly the same as it always did – people's faces, exactly the same.

'Listen,' said Don Antonio. 'Look at me, Charlotte.'

He was blurry. My head was pounding.

'The worst has happened. Nothing will be worse than this.'

And I knew he was right, because I wished that I did not exist, and in that moment I knew that I would never be afraid of anything – of saying anything, or doing anything, or being anything – ever again.

56. Drew

I had only been in Spain for a few days but everything was different. Going into school again felt like a prison visit. I wandered the halls, mentally saying goodbye to everything.

Mum and Dad didn't know. Nobody did. But I wasn't afraid. It was the right decision. I was an alien here.

I hadn't seen Charlotte all morning, but I heard some kids talking about her, giggling about the video, saying they'd seen her going into the principal's office with two cops. They were talking as if the police were there to arrest her rather than help her. I thought about saying something as I passed, but what can you say to people who don't understand anything? No. It wasn't them I had to talk to.

I caught sight of him from the window on the stairwell. He was alone, walking towards the clubhouse.

'Move!'

'Hey! Watch it! Oh ... sorry.' The young boy leapt out of my way as I bombed down the stairs.

His apology confused me until I remembered who I was supposed to be. I took the burgundy and gold S off my blazer and chucked it in the bin at the bottom of the stairs. I kept running. Past lockers, past the office, out of the front entrance, down the steps, across the playing fields.

'Adam!'

He turned around just as he reached the clubhouse, and as his face turned I caught him full force on the side of his cheek with my fist. I had never punched anyone before, and every time I had wanted to was concentrated in that strike. He stumbled backwards, mouth open in shock, and I rushed to push him down. Behind me I could hear people yelling in the distance. He was lying on his back clutching his elbow. I wanted to spit on him. I wanted to tell him everything I thought about him. But he looked pathetic. I hoped that he felt as small and helpless as he seemed. I turned my back to walk away. The people who'd been yelling were running across the field. One of them was Lucy. She shot me an icy glare.

'Worth it, was it?' she spat out, stopping in front of me and letting the others run to Adam's aid.

I didn't know what she meant.

She smiled but her mouth was a twisted line. 'You all think I'm so stupid and naïve,' she said. 'But the joke's on you.'

'What joke?' I said. 'None of this is funny. What are you talking about?'

'It was me,' she said, full of venom, jabbing at herself with her finger.

'What do you mean?'

'It was *me*. I told Adam that you'd cheated on me with Charlotte. I sent him the photo of you both. Why should you get to be a Steward when that's how you disrespect him?'

I knew she was angry and that she had a right to be angry, but my rage was still simmering from the punch and her words had only turned the heat up.

'Disrespect him? Charlotte doesn't *belong* to him, Lucy. I know we did wrong, but ... the video ... I mean, how can you think that's OK?'

Her eyes flashed pure rage. 'I *don't* think it's OK. I didn't know he had a video. Of course I didn't, because nobody tells me anything, do they? But I'm finding it hard to care right now. If any of you had been truthful with me it would never have happened. You're upset? She's upset? Why the hell should I care?'

She did care. I could hear it in her voice – the way it was faltering as she tried to keep up the aggression.

'Blame me,' I said. 'It was all my fault really. But Charlotte's your friend, and he ...' I looked over to where Adam was being helped to his feet by a couple of sixth-form girls. 'He doesn't care about anyone. He doesn't care about you either, Lucy. He didn't send that video out of loyalty to you.'

'What do you know about loyalty?' She wiped a tear from her face. 'You're an outsider and you always will be. I hate you.'

She ran off – small, light steps – sobbing. I watched her, unable to follow.

He'd sent the video because Lucy had showed him the photo of us. And she was so angry and hurt. I knew I should have been raging but all I could think of was that it was my fault. I'd taken away her allies so she'd turned to the most powerful person who could help her feel better. It was my fault.

I ran then but I didn't run back into the school. I would never set foot in there again. Instead I ran towards home. I didn't collect the stuff in my locker. It wasn't my locker any more. I didn't stop to wait for a bus or a train. I didn't want to stop. I knew where I had to be and I didn't want to stop until I got there. Until I got home. I ran until I felt like I was going to puke, but I still couldn't stop, so I walked as best I could, clutching the stitch in my side, and just as I thought I was going to collapse a car pulled over and the window came down and a voice shouted, 'Get in, you dickhead!'

I got in and Dale shook his head. 'Put the belt on and quit gurnin', fer God's sake.'

I hadn't realised that I'd been crying but when he said it I wiped my face and gulped the air, counting in the breaths to try to calm down.

'What's up?' he said.

But I couldn't say. I couldn't talk about any of it. I shook my head. Breathe. One, two, three, four. And out. One, two, three, four.

He kept his eyes on the road. 'So, you hear the news then?' he said.

I looked at him.

'It's a girl,' he said.

'What?'

'Karen. A wee girl. Yesterday morning.'

'Oh! Oh my God!'

He grinned widely. 'Never seen Jonny so happy in all his life. It came early. They were meant to be getting married in a couple of weeks.'

By the time we'd reached our estate I was almost able to breathe normally. I turned to him to tell him sorry, to ask him, again, to forgive me, but I still couldn't speak. He pulled over near my house.

'It's OK,' he said.

I had never wanted to hear two words more in my entire life. I didn't understand, though. How could it be OK? Nothing was OK.

'Chill, mate.'

I tried to smile but my breath was still coming out in little hiccups.

'Look. Jonny doesn't know about it. And him and Karen are totally happy right now. We all have to move on, don't we? Anyway, what's up with you? I take it you weren't running down the Lisburn road for the craic?'

I shook my head.

'We're still friends,' he said. 'Whatever's wrong, we're still friends.'

'Thanks,' I choked out. It sounded tiny and soft, but I meant it loudly.

'It's OK. Come out for cans later?'

'Yeah.'

57. Charlotte

If you'd told me at the start of the year that I'd have ended up sitting in Mr Baker's office with two police officers by the end of it I'd have laughed out loud. But sitting there, the office crowded with people, I felt like I'd never laugh again. Two police, Mr Baker, Don Antonio and, worst of all, my mum. All of them looking at me.

'Just take your time,' said Don Antonio quietly. 'Tell us what you told me in Granada. We're all on your side.'

'I'm so sorry, Mum,' I blurted out.

She looked so worried. She'd always said before that she was proud of me and that I was easy to look after because she knew she'd never have to worry about me doing the right thing. And here I was, doing the right thing, making her look so anxious that she looked like an old woman. I thought about what Don Antonio had said on the plane – that nothing would ever be as bad again – and I wondered if telling it would be worse. But it wasn't.

I made the words as clear as I could. I did not look at the floor. I looked at my mum. When the police asked me questions I looked at them. I did not cry because, for the first time, I did not feel ashamed. Just tired. So tired. Everybody knew now. And some of them not only knew, but they had *seen* as well. Mum squeezed my hand and said, 'It's OK, it's OK,' as if it was a spell.

And Don Antonio took my other hand and said, 'You are brave,' and I believed it, because that is what I had left: belief.

Whatever was inside, whatever nobody else could see, it was mine.

58. Drew

September

The rusty old swings creaked back and forth as we stood against them, rocking with our feet on the ground.

'Do you have to repeat the year, then?'

'Nah. I can do my A levels at the tech. They're following the same curriculum. Took me all summer to catch up the bits they'd done that we hadn't covered but it should be OK.'

'Do you miss it?'

'What, Cooke's?'

Charlotte laughed because it was a joke question. Of course I didn't miss Cooke's. I missed Don Antonio's classes but he'd left and gone back to Madrid.

'Fancy a chip?'

'Yes, I'm starving.'

We let the swings fall away and started making our way to the chip van on the edge of the estate. We were going to take the chips to the rec and eat them on the bench, just like we'd been doing every Thursday since I left school, and then she'd go home and later she'd text and we'd chat about nonsense or send stupid memes. The estate was full of crunchy brown leaves that would get soaked overnight and make everyone slip in the morning. We scrunched through them, anticipating the warmth of the food. The van was glowing like a church on the other side of the grass but we walked around the outside instead of cutting across in case of dog poo. There was a queue but I didn't mind.

Adam had been cautioned by the police. Charlotte's mum had started to take legal action, but Charlotte asked her to stop. She didn't want to end up in court having to go through it all again. The cops had taken his phone and computer and they found a whole pile of stuff – other videos of girls in our year, the stuff about Charles's marijuana shed, Adam's bank statements proving that he'd paid for my trip and not Don Antonio. But they said none of it was enough to prosecute him. He claimed everything had been consensual. He hadn't shared the other videos and nobody wanted to go up against him in court, knowing that his dad was a top barrister.

But he did leave school. Not long after I did. He wasn't kicked out, mind you. The principal didn't have the balls for it. He said that if the police didn't arrest Adam for anything then his hands were tied. The star rugby player was allowed to stay. But he left anyway. He left because he was finished.

A week after I'd left school and Charlotte had been interviewed by the police she called me.

'Charlotte. How are you?'

I heard her take a breath.

'I'm OK, actually. I mean, it's a nightmare being in school. But I'll be OK.'

'I'm really sorry,' I said. 'About everything.'

'It's OK.'

'It's not.'

'Look, Drew.' She sounded different. Determined. 'It's over and I need ...' Her voice wobbled slightly, but she coughed and corrected it. 'I need your help with something.'

A couple of days later we sat in the library on the Ormeau road and drew up a public statement. We wrote it again and again: first listing everything and everyone, then taking out anything unnecessary, then making sure we had the main points first. Then we wrote it again. We read it out loud. We imagined others reading it, imagined their reactions. When it was finished it was just 150 words long. It read:

An Open Letter to the Students and Staff at Cooke's Academy

Everyone is talking about it, but everyone is afraid to speak.

A teacher has left. A student has left. Another student has been humiliated.

Laws and hearts have been broken.

Everyone is talking, spreading rumours, but everyone is afraid to speak about the things we all know are true.

We know what happens at this school. We know who the powerful people are. But we are the ones who give them power. They have abused us.

We are calling on everyone who has been abused. Stop gossiping about other people. Speak about yourself and your experiences. Speak to your friends. You know you're not alone now. You've seen what has been done. But we know there's more. Much more. Tell your friends. Tell the police. When we all do it then we become the powerful ones.

We believe you.

When we were finished we photocopied the statement 200 times, and the next day Charlotte went to school early and posted them into people's lockers, pinned them on the noticeboards, left them around on the tables in the cafeteria.

Neither of us knew what would happen next, but what did happen was that the girls in our year stopped talking to Adam and started talking to one another. It took a few weeks, but when Adam lost the girls he began to lose kudos with younger boys, and as they resigned, one by one, from Steward servant duties, the Stewards also began to resign. Not formally. They'd just leave a badge lying around so people could see it discarded, and they'd begin to sit apart from Adam at lunchtime. Within a few weeks his dad had allegedly told Mr Baker that the school wasn't good enough for his son and he'd disappeared off to a fee-paying school up the country.

Now in my estate, months later, Charlotte ordered chips for us both and two tins of Coke. The drinks were freezing and the chips were roasting. When we got to the rec and ripped the bags open – the vinegar-soaked steam made our faces damp and we wiped them with hard chip-van napkins.

'Vinegar facial. My favourite,' said Charlotte, laughing. 'Hey – I forgot to tell you. Guess who asked about you today?'

'Who?'

'Lucy.'

'She … is she talking to you again?'

Charlotte nodded, mouth full of chip.

'Oh, that's great!'

'It was Artie's doing. He did a sort of mediation thing that he'd learnt on his summer law course. I think he just wanted to practise on us, really. But who cares, it worked.'

'So you're good now?'

'Well, kind of. It's early days. But I *think* she'll forgive me.'

'Amazing!'

'It is.'

I was honestly glad about it, although the mention of Lucy had brought back the memory I had been trying not to entertain. That night in Granada – the kiss; us walking down the hill from the cave, hand in hand. We had never talked about it. But maybe we didn't need to. She was here. With me. Like she was every Thursday. That was enough for now.

Epilogue

I wasn't sure about university any more. Mum and Dad wanted me to go, said they'd been saving up and that I could take a loan out, and that just killed me because my whole life they'd been telling me to never take out a loan or a credit card – to owe nobody anything. They didn't even like relatives lending us a few quid. It was a big thing for them to even think about borrowing money, never mind thousands of pounds. I hated to think about that scholarship and who would get it now. And then one day in the summer, just a few weeks after I'd left school, a parcel arrived at our house.

It was massive and addressed to me. We all stood there in the living room looking at it, trying to guess what it was. It was almost as big as my mum.

Finding out what was inside didn't make us any less confused. It was a guitar. Looked like an old one. It was an orangey colour and it smelt like tobacco or burning turf. It had a wide neck and a round body.

Dad picked it up. 'Givus a look!' He used to play when he was younger. 'Oh, this is a nice one, Drew,' he said, turning the knobs to tune it. 'Who sent you this?'

I searched through the packaging and found an envelope. I read the note.

'Who's it from, Drew?' said Mum.

I passed the note to her and Dad.

Dear Drew,

I hope you will forgive the extreme liberty I have taken to contact you and to send this gift. As you know, I resigned from the Henry Cooke Academy last term, and I am now in Madrid with my family. I intend to read a lot. I intend to write. I will consider teaching again, because, truthfully, I love it.

Last year my father died, and he left this guitar to me. I have spent some time wondering what to do with it. I don't play and I don't have any children. Drew, I wanted you to have it, because you have the *duende* Lorca spoke of. You have a rare talent for languages and I want you to develop the sense of yourself that you cannot yet completely fathom. Perhaps you will learn to play this guitar and take it with you to university. Lorca said it's useless to try to silence the guitar – we can't silence it. Wherever you go, you must try not to silence yourself. Keep on writing, whatever you do, but I hope that you will find your voice in further study at college.

Please let me write a reference for your application.

Cariñosos saludos,

Antonio Pérez Fernandez

We hope you have enjoyed reading *Grapefruit Moon*. On the following pages you will find out about some other Little Island books you might like to read.

Little Island

Books create waves

The Eternal Return of Clara Hart

by Louise Finch

A sensational YA debut about toxic masculinity and gendered violence.

Wake up. Friday. Clara Hart hits my car. Go to class. Anthony rates the girls. House party. Anthony goes upstairs with Clara. Drink. Clara dies. Wake up. Friday again. Clara Hart hits my car. Why can't I break this loop?

A flicker in the fabric of time gives Spence a second chance. And a third. How many times will he watch the same girl die?

Praise for *The Eternal Return of Clara Hart*	Awards

Praise for *The Eternal Return of Clara Hart*

"Compulsively readable"
– *The Guardian*

"I am glad this superb book exists"
– *The Irish Times*

"A devastating, essential journey"
– *Kirkus*, starred review

"Bold and honest"
– *The National*

Awards

Shortlisted for the Yoto Carnegie Medal for Writing 2023

Shortlisted for the Branford Boase Award 2023

Shortlisted for the Great Reads Award 2023

Shortlisted for the Badger Book Award 2023

Shortlisted for the YA Book Prize 2023

THINGS I KNOW

By Helena Close

Things I know. I'm a bad person.
I miss Finn. I could easily be a murderer.

Saoirse can't wait to leave school – but just before the Leaving Cert her ex-boyfriend dies by suicide. Everyone blames Saoirse, and her rumbling anxieties spiral out of control.

Saoirse feels herself flailing in swirling waters that threaten to suck her into the depths. No-one can save her – not her lovely nan; not the gorgeous boy who tries hard to love her; not her fabulous best friend; and certainly not her cheap-wisdom counsellor.

Can Saoirse, against all odds, rescue the self she used to know?

'Read it – and buy a second copy to thrust into the hands of the next platitude-utterer you encounter.'
The Irish Times

'An accurate portrayal of a young person's challenges, this book is also full of hope, love and laughter.'
The Sunday Independent

THE GONE BOOK

By Helena Close

Winner: White Raven Award 2021

Shortlisted: Dept 51 @ Eason Teen and Young Adult Book of the Year, Irish Book Awards 2020

Nominated: The 2021 Carnegie Medal

I know you'll hate me. But I can't help it.
I'm going to find you.

Matt's mam left home when he was 10. He writes letters to her but doesn't send them. He keeps them in his Gone Book, which he hides in his room. Five years of letters about his life. Five years of hurt.

Matt's dad won't talk about her. His older brother is mixed up with drugs. His friends, Mikey and Anna, are the best thing in his life, but Matt keeps pushing them away.

All Matt wants to do is skate, surf, and forget. But now his mam is back in town and Matt knows he needs to find her, to finally deliver the truth.

'This is as real as writing gets. Every line rings perfectly true.'
Donal Ryan

'A skillful and truthful novel from a wonderful storyteller.'
Joseph O'Connor

'Achingly sad but hugely funny. A gritty story full of heart.'
Sheena Wilkinson

NEEDLEWORK

By Deirdre Sullivan

Winner: Honour Award for Fiction,
Children's Books Ireland Awards 2017

Ces longs to be a tattoo artist and embroider skin with beautiful images. But for now she's just trying to reach adulthood without falling apart.

Powerful, poetic and disturbing, *Needlework* is a girl's meditation on her efforts to maintain her bodily and spiritual integrity in the face of abuse, violation and neglect.

'Reading Needlework is similar to getting your first tattoo – it's searing, often painful, but it is an experience you'll never forget.'
Louise O'Neill

'Needlework is a powerful novel that deserves to be read.'
Sarah Crossan

'A novel that is just as sharp and precise as its title suggests.'
Doireann Ní Ghríofa

Acknowledgements

My heartfelt thanks to the following humans:

Alfonso Salazar, for permission to use the line from Javier Egea's beautiful poem. *Muchas gracias*.

My agent, Jenny Savill, for believing in this novel and helping it to find its place.

Little Island, whose books I've been reading for years – I am so pleased to have been published by you. Thank you, Matthew, for giving this story a chance. To the classest/classiest/most class editor, Siobhán – thank you so much! Also, Kate, Elizabeth, Emma and Rosa: it has been a huge privilege to work with you.

Ana Jarén, for the amazing cover art, and Anna Morrison for the brilliant design.

The Arts Council of Northern Ireland, who funded the research and writing of this book.

My New York tour guide and emotional support manimal, Peterson Toscano.

Paul Magrs and Jeremy Hoad – for making me so welcome and for sweary uplifts.

Lots of love to my writing group, who are enormously good humans.

Sheena Wilkinson – you have been so generous in your support of my work.

Stephen Donnan-Dalzell, aka Cara Van Parke, the best-looking beta reader. Thank you, also, for naming my queen.

Ian Gibson, for teaching me about Lorca and introducing me to the word 'telluric'.

My kids, for their honesty and humour. J, thank you for the *bueno*.

And finally, thank you to my husband, Ian McMillan, for being my guide and translator in Granada, and for putting up with my affair with Lorca. Very tolerant of you. X

ABOUT THE AUTHOR

Shirley-Anne McMillan is a writer from Northern Ireland. She has worked as a teacher, an Online Writer in Residence for the Irish Writers Centre, a youth worker with LGBTQ young people and a creative writing tutor. She lives in Co. Down with her family and in her free time she loves playing the guitar and knitting.

ABOUT LITTLE ISLAND

Little Island is an independent Irish press that publishes the best writing for young readers. Founded in 2010 by Ireland's first children's laureate, Siobhán Parkinson, Little Island books are found throughout Ireland, the UK and North America, and have been translated into many languages around the world.

RECENT AWARDS FOR LITTLE ISLAND BOOKS

Spark! School Book Awards 2022: Fiction ages 9+
Wolfstongue by Sam Thompson

Book of the Year
KPMG Children's Books Ireland Awards 2021
Savage Her Reply by Deirdre Sullivan

YA Book of the Year
Literacy Association of Ireland Awards 2021
Savage Her Reply by Deirdre Sullivan

YA Book of the Year
An Post Irish Book Awards 2020
Savage Her Reply by Deirdre Sullivan

White Raven Award 2021
The Gone Book by Helena Close

Judges' Special Prize
KPMG Children's Books Ireland Awards 2020
The Deepest Breath by Meg Grehan